Sign up for our newsletter to hear
about new and upcoming releases.

www.ylva-publishing.com

THE
LAVENDER
LIST

BY MEG HARRINGTON

PROLOGUE

THE WAR'S OVER ON PAPER. Unless the combatant is a spy, an intelligence officer, or a shady diplomat. Those men and women, people like Laura Wright, never stop fighting. They're hunting down war criminals, rebuilding nations, and crowning new rulers.

Except for Laura, pre-eminent spy and leader of one of the deadliest Maquis groups in France. She's stuck managing security at a half-empty bomb factory overlooking the Hudson. The factory is in the midst of layoffs. Every day another locker is emptied, and Laura looks through the purses of exhausted and furious girls to make sure they're not taking any secrets with them.

It's not the war she set out to wage.

Her war ended a little after V-E day. British and American troops lumbered through the village she had called home for the last few years and declared it liberated. The members of the resistance cell she forged were heroes, and she was asked to return quietly to America.

"You did good work," her superiors said. As if killing over a hundred Nazis and being one of the most wanted spies in all of Europe was the same as *paperwork*.

Upon her return home, Laura found that her unique—and varied—skill set wasn't in demand. "Is that why you took the job?" Michel asked one night over coffee in a diner. Michel has never seen the point of her taking on a job now that the war's over—though he's eager to help her in any way he can.

Laura smiled into her drink. "Keeps me out of trouble, Michel. And it might be minding a factory, but it's one full of *bombs*."

He laughed. "You do love an explosively good time."

Laura rolled her eyes, because it was easier than flicking crumbs off her plate at him.

"It could be exciting, you know. More importantly it will keep me busy. Which is something I desperately need right now."

That had been a low blow, and Michel had wilted a little when she said it. Sipped his coffee and looked sullenly over her shoulder and out the window.

But it turns out, when no one is dropping the things, the demand for bombs plummets. As does the demand for stealing or sabotaging them.

The last three months have been particularly dull. Not even a trespasser. Just the steady stream of laid off girls filing out the door and Laura's own long nights quietly bemoaning her awfully boring lot in life over strong coffee at the diner.

It changes with a phone call.

She was chummy with Todd before the war. He's the intellectual sort who wears a lot of tweed and always has the cleanest fingernails. His cleverness and education kept him out of the fight and in the backrooms where his silver tongue and sharp eyes worked wonders.

Now, while she minds the unemployed and trains security guards in New York City, he's living in a villa in Italy and hunting down old Nazis.

"I loathe *and* despise you," she says, wrapping the phone cord around her finger.

Todd's laugh is obnoxious and airy over the line. "I've been having a good run," he says.

"So, Todd, darling, what are you calling about?" Giggling girls scamper by on Laura's hall.

He chuckles. "Never mind me. Where on earth are you living, Laura Wright?"

"A hotel. For women. Very popular in big cities. Keeps all us girls safe from nasty influences. Cheap too."

"And utterly wasted on me."

"I'm sure," she murmurs. "The only reason you ever want to chat, Todd, is when you have or want something. Which is it today?"

"Bit of both dear. You know how things have been since they axed the OSS." The OSS, before Truman executed it like a foreign spy, had been Laura and Todd's official employer. Espionage agents less rigid than the stuffed suits of the War Department. She'd have dared to call it home if she were ever to call a place that.

She idly wrapped the phone's cord around her finger. "My bank account is familiar."

"Everyone's going through Dulles and the State Department, and those men are—"

"Brutes."

"The only other game in town is... less adored by those above us."

"And which gaggle of ghastly men are paying for your new lifestyle Todd?"

3

"Very much the latter. It's why I'm calling. I need someone outside Dulles's purview. You know the kind? People with tact?"

"You could call anyone of my sex, Todd. Dulles and his cronies tend to avoid us all."

"I know. His loss. But I'd prefer you on this Laura. You've got a reputation."

She gives him her flirty laugh—even though they both know it's wasted on him. "What kind?"

"The best kind in our line of work. Particularly for something like this. You just need to go to a club. Use those wiles."

Laura hums in mock understanding. "I see. A little Rita Hayworth and it's all done."

"A little Rita. Perhaps some Kate Hepburn too. You see, someone has a package that we need, and they probably won't want to give it to you."

There's a dirty joke Laura could make, but Todd's far too refined to find it funny. So Laura taps her finger on the handle of the phone. "Of course. They never do."

"It will be easy." Todd is trying to assure her—like a good handler giving a rotten assignment should. "You'll just pop in and out. As simple as picking up your laundry."

It is, in fact, not that simple at all.

CHAPTER 1

AMELIA'S DAY WAS ABOUT AS rotten as the garbage she was stuck ferrying to the back of the alley. The big dumb ape her boss calls the cook stubs his toe, and goes *splat* right into the griddle. His hand gets burned so bad the other waitress says she's gonna ralph, and the boss kicks all the customers out with an apology and a weak smile. Amelia gets clean-up duty *and* closing duty because the other girl is as green as their uniforms and the boss wears a tie. No fella in a tie is gonna sack up the trash or wipe down the griddle. No siree.

While she cleans up, Amelia glances at the entrance more than she maybe should. She didn't see Laura at breakfast that morning and was kinda hoping—as stupid as it may be—that her neighbor might stop by for a slice of pie after work.

Laura's one of the last girls still on at a factory near the docks, and Amelia's diner is on the same train line back to the hotel. So, it isn't entirely stupid to think she might slip in for something tasty on her way home. Amelia even left a slice of chocolate meringue out. Seeing as the boss had already left for the night, she could let Laura in and everything.

She gets all these mental pictures of how it would be. Her cleaning and gabbing and Laura sitting on the stool by the window, with her blonde curls haloed in the blue light of the city and those long legs crossed at the knee. She'd purse her red lips, look at the pie, and consider. "It really is too large for just one person, Amelia."

And she'd grin and say, "Eat up, Laura."

Laura's got a sharp quality to her voice. That way of talking like Kate Hepburn—sounding as if she's the smartest gal in any room. Carries herself that way, too, with this cocky attitude that's at odds with the stylish looking dresses and jackets she wears. Laura Wright's a big bundle of addictive inconsistencies. But gosh golly she's got a nice smile. The kind that just warms a girl up from toe to top.

Amelia doubles down on scrubbing the griddle because, let's face it, girls aren't supposed to get all warm while thinking about another girl's smiles. Not when they're firmly in adulthood, and the close, bosom-buddy girlfriend feelings are reserved for doing each other's nails before a date with a big galunk of a guy.

She cleans the griddle until she can almost see her face in it, and Laura still doesn't show. Same after she mops. And after she wipes down every countertop.

She leaves the pie alone while she sacks up the trash.

So, Laura isn't gonna show up and split a piece of chocolate pie with her. Who cares! She'll finish her work—and finish her pie—and still be home before curfew. Unlike Laura, who can't even bother to show up at her friend's work, just to gab and walk home in the damp.

Outside, in the ally, the night's not too warm, but it's muggy. The fog rolled in and everything is… moist, but not wet enough to have to use her umbrella on her walk to the train. It's clingy, like a bad date, and there's just enough to the mist to make nasty little puddles. She shivers and side steps to keep from ruining her company-issued shoes on her way to the trash.

She's so busy watching for those murky pools in the alleyway, she almost misses the figure lurking in the shadows like a creep.

Almost.

Most gals stuck in a dead end alley with a creep would run. If she pressed to the wall and screamed the whole time she'd probably get free of the lurker. But Amelia's had a rotten day and she's holding on to a bag of trash heavier than a pillowcase full of door knobs.

She hefts her bag of trash over her shoulder like a weapon. "Come on out," she says, in a way she hopes to hell sounds forceful.

But the figure, instead of stepping out, slides down the wall and hits the ground like a sack of potatoes.

The light reflects off blonde hair, and Amelia squints, trying to figure out who it is. "Laura?"

Laura is as white as a sheet and half-conscious.

Amelia creeps closer and watches the ragged way Laura breathes. Kinda like when her little sister got the flu back in twenty-eight and her last breath had just rattled out.

She drops the trash on the other side of Laura, shielding the both of them a little from the street, and reaches out to touch her face.

Cool. Clammy. "Laura," she whispers. Part of her is curious about Laura's predicament, but most of her, worried.

Laura's dark eyes flutter open. They're mahogany brown, like fancy furniture that's been polished to a shine. Tonight, though, they are cloudy with confusion. "Amelia," she finally whispers. Her voice is thick.

Amelia cups her face, as if her own cold hands can transfer a little warmth. "Hey, how's your night going?" she says, and she manages to stop herself from adding a "kiddo." "Because you know, the last guy who used the backdoor got hit upside *his* backdoor with a broom."

Laura sort of smiles—a weak kind like a kid sick with a fever. Then she laughs, but it goes into a little bit of a wheeze. Amelia leans back on her heels, letting a little more light over her shoulder so she can see Laura better.

She hunches down and carefully tilts Laura's head. "You're hurt!"

Laura pats her hand. "I bumped my head at work. I think…" She sighs. "It might be more severe than I originally thought."

"You think? You must have bled down twenty blocks!"

She smirks. "Twenty-two."

Amelia is unimpressed. "Is now really the time to be crackin' wise?"

The smirk falls away. "I guess not."

"Come on. Let's get you inside, call a cab and get you to the hospital."

She reaches for Laura's arm to pull her up, but Laura pulls away. "I…"

"You what?"

"I can't afford a doctor."

Amelia stares. "What're they paying you with down at the bomb factory?" She refrains from asking the more prudent question, that is, why's a girl who clearly comes from money—the job's obviously Laura's stab at independence from her family—so broke she can't afford a doctor?

Laura's grin is saucy. "Brandy and—" She winces, and Amelia only feels a little sorry for her. "Right. No jokes. Bad timing. I did—I did call someone. To help."

"And you thought you'd wait for 'em in the alleyway outside my work?"

"I kind of hoped to make it inside. I just got… waylaid."

"Because you got your clock cleaned! How the heck does that even happen to an office girl?"

"Floor's not the only dangerous place in the factory."

Amelia tries to laugh it off with a bad joke. "Yeah, staplers and hole punches. Real dangerous."

That's when Laura looks at her all earnest, which isn't a thing Laura does often. The few times Amelia's seen her do it, it's kinda like watching that wolf all dressed up in granny's clothes. But this time it feels genuine, as if she doesn't just want, but *needs* Amelia—and only Amelia—to believe her.

"I really didn't think it was as bad as this when I left."

Damn it, Amelia thinks. She sighs. "Any idea how long until your pal gets here?" She's got a good idea who the friend will be. There's a fella who sits close to her in the diner and pretends they aren't talking to each other, that they don't know each other backward and forward.

Black hair, perpetual stubble.

Handsome.

Fancy, in his expensive suits and silk ties.

French.

Laura looks down at her watch, the face rotated around to the inside of her wrist, and reads the time. "He's always been very punctual. So I would imagine any moment—"

The bright lights of a car dazzle the both of them. Laura shields her eyes and hisses in annoyance. Amelia stands and reaches for the trash bag as if she's gonna throw it at the car. Laura's cool fingertips on her bare ankle stops her.

"It's all right," she says. "That's my friend."

Sure enough it *is* the friend. Tall, Dark, and French.

"Sacre—Laura!" He stumbles out of the car. Then stops and rights himself, taking the time to smooth back his hair.

Then he does that thing he always does—smiles politely and ignores her. Fella's only got eyes for Laura, and Amelia can't blame him. It's the legs. And the splash of red she wears on her lips. And that coy quality to her smirk. And the way she looks at Amelia—

Jumpin' Jehosohaphat, the guy talks a lot of French. Enough that Amelia's waiting for him to pop a baguette out of his pocket and then bend over for the Germans.

Laura seems to understand it and is kinda blasé about the whole thing. Tall, Dark, and French is very… animated, and his hair keeps falling into his eyes as he pokes and prods Laura as if he's her Tall, Dark, and French nurse. He jerks her head to the side and gasps at the sight of blood, and then brushes his own particularly foppish locks back out of his eyes again.

Laura just nods along with what sounds like a rant. Or maybe a plan? Laura says some of her own stuff in French, and the words spit out of her mouth like bullets from a gun. Then they both seem to remember Amelia's still standing there, awkwardly clutching her bag of trash like an old lady clutches her purse.

Two sets of dark eyes fall on her and Amelia feels as if she's stuck in the headlights of Tall, Dark, and French's car.

She hops forward. "Amelia Maldonado," she says. She offers her hand and Tall, Dark, and French just looks at it then gives her a tight smile that must be French for "I do not care."

"If she's game, perhaps you can patch me up, and Amelia can take me home," Laura says, officially bringing the conversation back into English.

"Sure, I mean, if you think you'll be okay. I had a cousin one time who didn't get a cut checked out on his leg and now..." She makes a cracking noise in the side of her mouth. "No leg."

Tall, Dark, and French smiles congenially. "I assure you, Laura will retain the use of all her faculties. And," he says as an afterthought, "her leg." It sounds a little sultry the way he says it. His accent tinges his words but doesn't overwhelm 'em, like some Charles Boyer fella trying to seduce Irene Dunne.

It rankles the heck out of Amelia. As bad as that mouth of his, uttering Laura's name. Wrapping his lips around it as if it's a candy to be savored.

They move Laura to the back of his spacious car, Amelia's hand around one awfully firm bicep and Tall, Dark, and French's holding up Laura's other hand. That big graceful looking hand of his is all comfortable at the small of Laura' back.

He gets Amelia to hold up the light so he can examine the cut, which is bloody and long but not so bad when a person can actually see it. Tall, Dark, and French's clever fingers quickly clean and stitch it as if he's darning a pair of pants.

Laura doesn't even flinch. Just looks straight ahead. Maybe glances at Amelia once. But turns away before Amelia can catch her eye.

Amelia, for her part as assistant, manages to not retch at the sight. Though, between this and the cook's sautéed hand, she can probably skip a meal or two now.

Then Tall, Dark, and French purses his lips. "And your chest?"

Amelia's eyes must bug ten feet out of her head. But Tall, Dark, and French is devoted to his patient and his patient is devoted to sighing. "It's not so bad."

"You've harmed your ribs, dear. It's rather obvious. Otherwise you wouldn't be wheezing like that windbag I call an uncle. You know the one. Hates stairs."

Laura glances at Amelia. "A door hit my... chest." Amelia can't stop one of her eyebrows from climbing up toward her hairline. "It was a very large door," Laura continues feebly. "With a... knob."

"Like a fist," Tall, Dark, and French mutters.

Amelia agrees with him, silently. She hopes her look gets across that she wasn't born yesterday and if Laura wanted to be honest then Amelia would welcome it.

Laura ignores 'em both. She huffs and then is very perfunctory with the unbuttoning of her shirt, and it gives both Amelia and Tall, Dark, and French access to all kinds of skin and black underthings that usually require a couple of meals and a drink or two first.

Amelia tries not to flush and pays lip service to finishing up and clocking out while they work. She thinks she hears light laughter on her way back into the diner. The two of them chuckling at the big queer joke that's Amelia Maldonado.

She's probably imagining it. And that's what she tells herself as she shuts off every light in the diner and rummages through the drawers in the office to find the keys for the front door.

Laura's a lot of things, but she's not sitting out in that car with some kind of—of *boyfriend* just yukking it up over Amelia not being in on their little French joke.

Amelia jerks the key a little too hard in the back door when she locks it, and then pulls her flimsy raincoat tighter around herself. It's totally worthless after all her time in the back alley, but it feels like a little protection when she marches up to Tall, Dark, and French and demands he drive her and Laura home.

He looks surprised. His eyebrows flying up into his hairline. "You wouldn't prefer a cab?" he asks, his accent's thick, but Amelia can still hear the sarcasm in it.

"Michel," Laura growls from the backseat. She's all hidden in shadows, just one pale hand in the light. "Don't be an ass. We've got curfew at ten, and I'd really rather not give Mrs. Myrtle another reason to glower at me." Amelia's not the biggest expert of the human condition—despite her acting teachers telling her she should be. But she can still tell "Michel" is annoyed. Still, the guy's nice enough to hold the door open for Amelia, as she climbs into the backseat of his fancy car that costs more than her yearly rent. She knows a thing or two about cars—enough to know his is outrageously expensive.

"How's a guy afford a car like this?" she asks him when they're on the road. She doesn't get to sit in a car much nowadays and it's pleasant. And it's a much smoother ride than she remembers, too.

Cars she used to drive went too fast and made her teeth rattle.

Tall, Dark, and French stares back at her using the rearview mirror, and she can only see his eyes, hard and cool, in the reflection. It's maybe the first time he's ever really looked at her. "It's not my car, chere."

She glares right back. "Whose is it?"

"Why do you want to know?"

"My friend shows up bleeding on my doorstep, so I'm a little curious." Her "friend" is currently passed out beside her, and the weight of her head on Amelia's shoulder feels real nice.

"Your concern is noted."

And so is his lack of concern.

Laura sighs in her sleep, and Amelia resists the dumb urge to brush the hair off her face so she can get a better look.

"What'd you give her?" she instead asks softly. "Drugs?" She drops her voice an octave. "Booze?"

Tall, Dark, and French chuckles in a way that conjures up images of dark and smoky Parisian cafés. "Laura's tolerance is far better than yours or mine." Then he goes real tender. "And she really shouldn't have anything alcoholic with that lump forming on her head."

"She's gonna feel like a horse kicked her in the morning."

"She will."

"And she got hurt—"

"She was rushing a file to the other side of the office. The door stopped her."

It's the same as Laura's story, and as stories go, it's a pretty standard one. Especially for ladies who don't want people asking questions. No one pushes for explanations when "it was a door" or even some stairs.

But Amelia doesn't believe it. Not when she's seen Laura talking discreetly with this guy who drives an expensive car and patches Laura up as if he's been doing it all their lives. Not when she knows he thinks it was a fist too.

"She in trouble?" she asks, and she knows Tall, Dark, and French catches her drift. She's never exactly been in their particular world, but she's seen enough of it to know how to talk.

He's got the steel-eyed look again, tempered by just enough tenderness to put most folks off the trail. "I assure you, Miss Maldonado, she's not."

Amelia doesn't believe him, because she isn't the patsy he and Laura seem to think she is. She takes Laura's hand in hers and squeezes it.

Laura doesn't mumble, but her breath is hot on Amelia's neck.

They get to the hotel, and Tall, Dark, and French offers to help take Laura upstairs. Amelia levels a good glare at him. "She doesn't talk much about her home life does she?"

"Not enough." He smirks.

She bites back the smile that should accompany the nasty satisfaction she gets at chastising him. "No guys above the first floor. Especially not pimps patching up the girls."

He flusters and tries to hurriedly dissuade her, but Amelia's well and truly done with the guy, so she ignores him. She awkwardly leans all of Laura's weight onto her shoulder and pinches her as they walk toward the entrance. "I need you to wake up, Miss Wright. We got a job to do."

Behind them, Tall, Dark, and French calls her back but she shoots him the bird without looking up.

Laura shakes her head and slowly opens her eyes. Her head lolls as she looks back at Tall, Dark, and French and then toward Amelia. "What happened?"

"Your 'friend' brought us home. Now you got to pretend you're A-OK so we can make it up the stairs."

Laura half-salutes, and they march toward the entrance. Laura giggles loudly. Amelia's never heard her giggle. It's all... girlish. The kind of girlish giggle she and Laura usually roll their eyes at when they hear it tinkling around them at breakfast.

The Sebastian Hotel's got a decent breakfast, affordable rooms, and nice clientele, but it's also got one Edith Myrtle working the night shift. She's a wiry-haired widow who loves church, cross-stitch, and ferreting out bad girls.

She stops them halfway up the stairs with a terse cry of their names. It's worse than any what-for a mother would give. "You're home later than usual," she says, peering at them with beady eyes behind glasses as thick as the bottom of a pop bottle.

Amelia glances at the clock at the top of the stairs.

Ten past the hour. They broke curfew.

Amelia opens her mouth to spin God knows what, but Laura is faster.

"Oh Mrs. Myrtle," she honest to God sobs. "You will never believe what..." she sniffs, "what just happened."

Amelia listens as raptly as Mrs. Myrtle, because she's curious herself.

"Our train got stuck."

Mrs. Myrtle has not fallen for the stuck-train excuse in over a year. She's got a number for every damn train line in the city and can fact check that whopper faster than a cop.

"So naturally we had to disembark."

Amelia just nods. Laura's clearly working herself up to tell this story, and Amelia doesn't want to interrupt a fellow actress.

"But we were so far up town. Far too far away to make it back in time. Unless—"

Mrs. Myrtle leans in. Eyes behind her glasses wide.

"Unless we ran. Amelia was even ready to do it barefoot."

Mrs. Myrtle's eyes flicker over to Amelia as if she's forgotten she was there. Then down to her feet, which are, in fact, dirty from all the running around in the alley.

"But some men, well you know how much like dogs they can be."

The enthusiastic nod says Mrs. Myrtle does know.

"Well they saw us running and gave chase!"

"No!"

"Oh yes. Just flying after us! So Amelia, brave soul that she is just ran out into the street. Got us a cab. Didn't matter that we hadn't the money to pay for it. As long as we escaped the men."

Mrs. Myrtle is a big fan of bad spending if it means less men around, and gives Amelia a fond look.

"But I'm afraid the cab driver wasn't quite as kind as all that and we've been stuck out there all this time trying to convince him not to call the police on us."

"Should I go speak with him?"

Laura shakes her head sagely. "That won't be necessary. Amelia was *very* persuasive."

Did Laura have to lean on the *very* like that? It made Amelia sound like some kind of pugilist. Or prostitute. She wasn't really sure which.

It was the dumbest story Amelia'd ever heard, but Laura spun it like one of those breathless dolls on the radio, and somehow Mrs. Myrtle bought it. Hook, line, and sinker.

"You girls should rest," she says, and then she sends them both up the stairs and starts rubbing her hands together like she always does when she's downright *fraught*.

"Just carry that story up your sleeve," Amelia mutters out the side of her mouth as she lugs most of Laura's weight up two flights.

"For a rainy day," Laura agrees.

"Got any more of 'em? We could make a fortune selling them to girls on the hall."

Laura smiles sleepily. "I'll see what I can do."

On their floor, Laura becomes completely useless again, and Amelia has to prop her up against Laura's own door as she searches her for keys.

Laura stops her with a viselike grip on her wrist and produces the keys from her pocket, dangling them in front of Amelia. "Looking for these," she asks coyly, and it occurs to Amelia that Laura might actually be drunk. Or maybe she just gets flirty when folks knock her on the head.

She snatches the keys from Laura and holds her up with one hand around her waist while she uses the other to open the door. Laura's arms find their way around Amelia's shoulders and it's just…It's a hug.

Laura Wright, smelling like garbage, antiseptic, and that perfume that's always wafting out of her room, is hugging her. Amelia almost—*almost*—doesn't want to open the door.

But she does, and Laura steps back into the shadows of her room. As playful as she's been, it's all gone once she steps over that threshold.

"Thank you, Amelia." She's serious again.

So Amelia tries not to be serious. Even though she wants to follow her into that room, keep her safe, and send her back home on the first train to Connecticut if it will stop whatever's happening. "Take it easy Laura," she says with a crooked grin.

She tosses the keys at Laura's chest who catches them without blinking. Then she slowly closes the door. Leaving Amelia feeling like a caboose in the middle of the hallway.

She shuffles back into her own room. Hissing when she sees her ruined stockings and dirty shoes in the mirror. That'll be fun to clean up. Tomorrow. After she's had a good night sleep.

But after scrubbing her face, peeling off her clothes and climbing into bed in a shift she really ought to have laundered, she can't actually sleep.

Her stupid brain is turning over the night's events. Peering at 'em like a robber looking at the plans for a bank. Laura's just gone and told a whopper of a lie to Amelia (the one to Mrs. Myrtle doesn't count because *everyone* lies to Mrs. Myrtle).

And Amelia can't quite figure out why. Apart from insane theories about Laura being a lady of the night.

Tomorrow, she tells herself again. And she snuggles down under the covers and sighs.

She'll talk to Laura tomorrow. They'll sort it out and go right back to being pals who share smiles over the breakfast table and sneak bites of pie at the diner.

CHAPTER 2

THE NEXT MORNING LAURA LAUGHS off what happened and assures Amelia she's A-OK. She butters her toast and bites into it with relish. "I'm fine," she says. "It was just—an accident."

Amelia likes to think the look she gives Laura says she's no fool. But Laura must miss it because she steers the conversation away from their night with a wave of her butter knife.

As if Amelia can't see the line of stitches hidden in her hairline.

"Laura you're not the least bit—"

"It's fine, Amelia." She snaps. "*I'm* fine. Now let's talk about shoes. Because I think we should splurge sometime this week. I've repaired my heel three times in the last two months and I know you're needing a new pair. How about a trip up Fifth Avenue? Just the two of us?"

Things, for Laura at least, go back to normal. At least as far as Amelia can tell.

Laura comes to the diner, or she stops by Amelia's room to ask for a cup of sugar, or she invites her over for tea. At night, Amelia stares at her ceiling and wonders if maybe it was some crazy dream she had, because the way Laura's acting as if it never happened, really has Amelia questioning her own sanity.

Then she notices Laura's sneaking out and in most nights, wearing fancy dresses or coats so big they swallow her up.

"You okay?" Amelia asks.

And Laura waves her off with a smile that should be condescending, but really just sets loose a set of butterflies in Amelia's stomach.

A few more bruises take up residence on Laura. Little ones most folks won't notice. 'Cept the ones around her eyes, puffing 'em up on account of sleeplessness.

Amelia stops asking though. She's offered Laura every opportunity to own up, and instead the woman waves her off with an airy laugh and tells her it's all right.

Amelia tries to slot her into the category of "cute girl who won't last." It's a nasty category to have, but one Amelia's built out of necessity.

Then Tall, Dark, and French shows up at the diner, sits in the booth across from Laura, and looks up at Amelia like they're familiar with one another, saying, "Hello, Miss Maldonado."

Amelia pours him a cup of coffee and knows she can't categorize Laura so easily. The hot streak of jealousy that races up through Amelia at the sight of him is proof enough that Laura's more than some cute girl who won't last.

Amelia glares at Tall, Dark, and French, hoping just a nasty look can convey her hatred for him and whatever he's got Laura wrapped up in.

It works.

Tall, Dark, and French goes from breezy to shifty and ashamed.

Good.

Laura, not acknowledging either of them, leaves to go to the bathroom.

"I'm not what you think I am," he assures her in a low voice as soon as Laura's gone.

"Excuse me if I don't believe you," she assures right back, her whisper harsh.

"I—" He catches himself. It's like he wants to prove he's a good man. But a fella shouldn't have to work to prove it. He should just be. Amelia is wise enough to know this guy ain't. Not if he's using Laura.

She raises an eyebrow and waits for him to finish.

But he flushes and flusters. "You're misunderstanding the other night."

She leans in, one hand on her hip and the other holding the coffee pot too tight. "I really don't think I am, 'chere.'"

He presses his fingers into the laminate so hard they turn red under his fingernails. The 'chere' bit got to him. Serves the Frenchie right, sounding like Charles Boyer and looking like a stubbly Gregory Peck.

Still glaring at him, she lifts her chin. "What's your cut?"

His head snaps up, and he looks horrified. "It isn't like that."

"Yeah," she spits. "It is."

"Everything all right?" Laura's back.

Amelia spins on her heel, plasters on a big old smile, and says, "We're swell." Tall, Dark, and French swallows and nods.

She goes back to work, and the two of them sit there, looking like the lovers Laura's insisted repeatedly they aren't.

At least this time Laura doesn't smile when Tall, Dark, and French talks.

"Quickly," she hears him say. Like he's just given Laura marching orders she can't abide.

Amelia can just barely make out Laura saying in a low voice, "I don't want to do it."

Tall, Dark, and French tilts his head and looks apologetic. "We all have to do things we don't like, Laura."

A little later, he collects his things and leaves, stopping at the door to stare hard at Amelia. She stares hard back, never breaking eye contact, not even as she pours a cup of coffee for a harried mom with her yowling kid.

Laura's still sitting in her booth. Her mouth is small and tight in a frown. It dissolves when she notices Amelia watching her, and Amelia makes like she's looking away.

But she still watches Laura out of the corner of her eye. And the frown returns, changing Laura's face until her eyes are narrow in anger and she's taut like wire.

She gets up when she thinks Amelia's busy with another table, and Amelia stops long enough to watch her walk out. Laura's shoulders are rigid. Like she's got some bad news. Like maybe Tall, Dark, and French was telling her something she didn't want to hear. Maybe giving her a job she shouldn't have to take.

Damn it. Amelia knows what she's gotta do. She's got to go be nosey and investigate what exactly Laura does for a living.

And, if need be, she'll clean a dirty pimp's clock.

She figures the first thing she's gotta do, if she's gonna help Laura get loose of the nasty life she's leading, is figure out what the hell actually happened to Laura on the night she slumped her way into the alley. Amelia had been too insecure to pay attention when Tall, Dark, and French was patching Laura up, so she didn't get a good enough look at Laura's beating to have an idea of how she was hurt. The only thing she knows for sure is it wasn't a door.

Laura's sitting inside the diner, perched on a stool at the counter, gorgeous legs crossed and blonde hair perfectly coifed. Long fingers clutching a pen and jotting down notes in a pad. She doesn't comment when she sees Amelia get into an embarrassingly heated conversation with a twelve-year-old paperboy outside.

Though she definitely smirks when the kid kicks Amelia in the shin.

All because Amelia needs the kid to get her a week-and-a-half's worth of newspapers without gouging her like a freaking Wall Street suit.

"All right?" Laura asks when Amelia limps back inside.

"Kid kicks like a mule."

Laura laces her fingers together and balances her chin on them. "Lot of experience with those?"

"Loads of 'em past Atlantic Avenue. You didn't know?"

"I don't find my way that deep into Brooklyn often."

"You're pullin' my leg."

"I wish I were."

"Even Coney Island?"

She shakes her head.

"You don't know what you're missing. Hot dogs. Rides. Way better than anything you'd get up in Connecticut."

"Well, of course it is."

She rattles her leg real quick to get the last sting of the kick out of it. "Hang in there, Laura. You'll get there one day." It's as gentle a tease as Amelia can muster under the circumstances.

"That an invitation?" Laura fires back.

It's a joke, but there's heat in her words, and Amelia hopes Laura can't see her freeze. She swallows. "You want it to be?"

Laura's been looking down, writing some notes in a pad, and she looks up at that. Her dark eyes fall briefly on Amelia's mouth before she pegs her with a stare that'll haunt for a shameful night or two. But then she smiles. The heat is gone, and it really is just a joke. Nothing too sincere. It rarely is with Laura Wright.

That's A-OK for Amelia. Because those brief moments of belly-warming and knee-weakening sincerity between the bits of infuriating *in*sincerity are enough.

That twelve-year-old paperboy drops off a week-and-a-half's worth of newspapers at the Sebastian in a rucksack big enough that fellow Sebastian resident, Sarah Trellis, asks if there's a body in it.

She almost tells her it's her boyfriend, just to see Trellis fume, but doesn't. Knowing that cow, she'd want to see inside, and the whole hotel'd start worrying about Amelia hoardin' papers like that crazy old man that got crushed under twenty years' worth of cat hair and back issues of the New York Times.

The first thing she learns, ensconced in her room and armed with a bright light and a big pot of coffee, is that combing through a week-and-a-half's worth of papers for one of the largest cities in the world is boring. Back-aching and mind-numbingly boring. She can only go for twenty minutes at a time before she's pacing the rug her mom gave her into ruins and stretching like an alley cat.

The second thing she learns is that peering at newspaper print for hours on end is painful on the eyes. So, she stops, opens the window wide, leans out, and stares at the skyline instead.

The sun's setting and the sky's red. It hits the glass of all the buildings on the horizon and when a train, a truck, or even a big breeze rattles those windows, it's like the whole city is on fire.

It's a pretty sight, and Amelia rests her head on her fist and sighs. She sounds wistful. She ought to remember that exact sigh for the next audition.

The window to her right scrapes open and Laura sticks her head out. She doesn't look surprised to see Amelia there. If anything, it's like she was looking for her. Or maybe Amelia just imagines the softening around Laura's eyes when she catches her doing her best Juliet.

"It's Sunday," she says. "I thought you'd be in South Brooklyn visiting your family."

Amelia waves her off. "They see enough of me as is. I figured I'd take a day for me for a change."

She smiles. "I quite like that idea. Taking a day for yourself." She holds onto the window sill, pointedly staring at the skyline instead of Amelia.

"What about you," Amelia asks. "Taking a day?"

"There's no rest for the wicked."

Amelia laughs. It's too soft in her ears. "You're a lot of things Laura, but I'd never peg you as wicked."

Laura just murmurs.

Neither of them talk for a while. The sun sets slowly and the drone of a whole city tickles their ears. It's just the second floor, but even from this high up, it sounds less like a city and more like a river. A distant, cranky river with more than one timing belt in need of changing.

"How'd you know I was in," she eventually asks.

"I heard you pacing about. Everything all right?" Laura sounds genuine.

"Audition," she lies.

That catches her interest, and Laura perks up. "Need help? I played a mean Hamlet once upon a time."

"No foolin'?"

"Boarding school before the war." She shudders comically, but then smiles softly like she's got an old joke in her head. "Nothing worse than youths trying to be actors. Though a few have done well for themselves since."

Amelia grins. "You know famous folks, Laura Wright?"

"Oh, all sorts."

"Who? Specifically."

Laura's coy, and it feels, for a second, like before Amelia knew she was moonlighting as a prostitute. "That's in the past, darling."

Amelia sighs theatrically. "So's that time I shared an elevator with Greta Garbo."

"Did she 'just want to be alone'?" Laura draws her face down and affects a really bad accent for the impression, and Amelia has to roll her eyes.

"Jeez. That one's old enough to be my dad."

"You're quite developed for a ten-year-old."

"We bloom early in the Maldonado family."

"We were all late bloomers in the Wright family. Mother thought I'd never 'blossom.'"

Amelia snorts. Laura smiles again.

27

It's enough to almost forget that hazy look Laura had in her eyes when Amelia found her in the alley and the gajillion pounds of newspaper taking up space on her coffee table.

Almost.

"Hey Laura, you doing all right?"

Laura's still smiling and nods. "I've 'blossomed,' if that's what you're asking."

"It isn't."

Just like that, it's like someone's stuck a knife in their tires. Any fun whizzes out in a pathetic sigh.

"I'm all right," she says so seriously, attention still on that skyline.

"And your fella?"

"Amelia..."

She's gonna tell Amelia to leave it alone, and Amelia really doesn't want to hear that. "I worry."

"You mustn't."

"Wouldn't you?" God, she can sound like a real bitter hag when she wants to.

Laura, who always has a story, can't figure out what to say. Her jaw works, but nothin' comes out, so Amelia nods and shuts the window.

A minute later, there's a knock on her door, but she isn't in any mood to answer. Not when she's looking at a little blurb in the afternoon paper just a day after Laura's attack. One unidentified woman. Two men. One guy in the hospital, but the other guy and the woman are long gone.

She stares real hard at the name of the guy in the hospital. Then she looks up at her door and sees Laura's shadow under it. And she bites her lip and regrets every choice that's ever led her to this moment. Because the guy in the hospital?

That's her cousin.

CHAPTER 3

Laura's waiting for Amelia downstairs with a spot across from her saved. Just like they normally sit for breakfast. Cozy and content even in a room of other gals. But Amelia's worried. Laura's got a smile on her face and it's like she's gonna toss off that prickly coat of "massive asshole" she normally wears to—Amelia doesn't know—ingratiate herself.

Worm her way back into Amelia's good graces without even an apology or an acknowledgment of what's happened.

"We're making this a bad habit," Laura says, her eyes on her newspaper, but her tone is real teasing. Like they don't see each other every morning and most nights. Like a quiet breakfast between the two of them isn't the best part of either of their days.

"Real easy to break this habit," Amelia fires back.

Laura purses her painted lips. She looks around, and Amelia does, too. They're alone for the moment, but a group of girls are incoming, and their little bit of quiet morning paradise is about to go up in a gale of girlish glee.

"I don't do friends easily," Laura says urgently. "And I appreciate your patience, but—"

"But you're about as talkative as an OSS agent."

Laura jokes, "Hopefully less."

"See!" She catches her rising voice and glances guiltily around the room before hunching over the table and whispering, "See, that's what I mean. You'd rather joke than talk."

"I talk. We've talked, Amelia."

"Where was I born?"

"South Brooklyn," she snaps.

Amelia nods. "Yeah? Now ask me the same question. Guess what my answer would be?"

"New Haven," Laura ventures.

"Or Boston. Or Princeton. How would I know?"

"Neither of those are in Connecticut."

Amelia glares.

Laura looks down at her coffee and spins the cup on its saucer. The group of girls sit beside them and talk a mile a minute. Amelia butters her toast and listens lazily. Laura takes too big a bite of a biscuit and stares at Amelia while she chews it.

Even though Laura's been at the table longer, Amelia's the first one to leave. There really is an audition she could have spent her Sunday working on. Now the audition's after work and she hasn't prepped. If she clocks in early, maybe the boss'll let her go early, she hopes.

The click of heels on the tile tells her that Laura followed her out of the dining room and into the foyer.

"It's Hartford," she calls. She's being serious again, and Amelia has to stop walking or she might trip. "And I've got a family that cares for me, and I even have friends—spread across four continents, but I lost too much in that blasted war."

Amelia can see Laura's reflection in the glass of the front door. So serious and urgent, looking at the back of Amelia's head with the kind of intensity that could melt a girl. She means she lost someone.

Amelia turns carefully. "A friend? Or boyfriend."

Laura winces.

Amelia speaks softly—which is a chore for her. "How'd he go?"

Laura swallows, and it looks like she's on a razor's edge between her status quo and what the rest of the world calls feelings. "Nazi interrogation."

"I'm sorry."

One side of Laura's mouth crooks up. "I believe that's my line." She lifts her hand up, like she's gonna run it through her hair, catches herself, and lets it drop to the back of her neck. "Amelia...I told you, I'm not very good at being a friend."

"Yeah, you're pretty lousy at it."

"But I want to change." She starts to reach for Amelia's hand and stops and smiles in that friendly way that's never quite believable. "I happen to have a bottle of brandy that needs to be emptied."

"Yeah?"

Her hands are at her side, fidgeting like they need something to do. She takes a step toward Amelia. "I can't think of anyone better to share it with."

Amelia steps closer. There's about a sliver of light between them.

"That all you're sharing?" It comes right out of her. A reflex like kicking the doctor when he taps you on the knee. She can't believe she said it and holds her breath, waiting for Laura to say something back.

Laura, when she wants to be, is a damn cipher. "Tonight," she says, and Amelia can't tell if she's being set up or if Laura, standing so close she can smell her perfume, wants to kiss her.

She nods. "See you after work."

She doesn't get around to making the call she's gotta make until after the post-lunch rush. The boss steps out for a smoke and that leaves the broom closet he's christened his "office" empty.

The dial on his phone sticks on the three but she finally manages to get a call out to her cousin Al. He is, as one would expect after what the newspaper recounted, still in the hospital, but his wife seems to think he'll be okay.

"His skull got nearly cracked in half, but the doctors are saying he'll be talking real soon." Al's wife is the exact kind of optimistic idiot a fella like her cousin needs.

Then she tells Amelia to hold and doesn't bother covering the mouthpiece as she shouts across the room to Amelia's uncle that his niece is on the line and does he want to talk to her.

Amelia does not want to talk to her uncle, but if she hangs up, she'll wind up with a little, bald Italian man on her doorstep and her date that night'll be ruined.

If it is a date.

It might not be a date—

"Amelia, baby doll, it's been too long." Her uncle Vince got a voice that's smooth like that last drag of a cigarette. And he's the only man that she's never wanted to punch when he compares her to a toy.

"Hi," she says. 'Round him, she always has trouble finding more than three words to put together. There's a kind of menace to her uncle. He's the guy that slaps kids for having a smart mouth and can turn a grown man mute with a glare.

"You're calling after Alfonso?"

"I saw his name in the paper."

He hems and haws about his son and then invites her to come visit him. He misses her. He'd like to see her.

You don't turn down a fella like Vince Pedrotti. Ever.

She tries. "Well I got an audition tonight…"

"So tomorrow." Vince Pedrotti doesn't make requests. He says something and it happens. He'd tell the moon to rise at noon, and there it'd be, shining in the sky.

"I—"

"You can come after work, can't you?"

She can. She doesn't really want to, but she can. Phone still pressed to her ear, she thumps her head against the wall and wonders, again, why she thinks she needs to save Laura Wright.

"Yeah," she finally says. "I'll see you tomorrow."

The back door of the diner slams open, and she hangs up fast, slipping out of the closet before the cloud of pomade and cigarette smoke she calls a boss can see her.

The audition, from Amelia's view, does not go well. Something about staying up all night reading old newspapers. Something about thinking about her family and about her next door neighbor, left Amelia so distracted that she starts by reading the other person's lines.

Twice.

Her head and feet and everything in between aches by the time she clomps up the stairs to her room. Girls say hello and Sarah Trellis tries to talk to her like they're friends, and she's proud of herself for not shoving her over the banister.

The lights are out in Laura's apartment. Hayseed is coming out of her room on the opposite side of Laura's. Her real name's Judy something, but Amelia's not keen to remember because the gal's not real likely to make it more than a month. She smiles at Amelia all big and wide the way only people who've never seen the Atlantic can.

Amelia plasters on her biggest, broadest smile, nods, and says "yeah" a lot as the girl talks about how *big*! and *exciting*! everything is in New York City.

"Have you seen Laura," she asks, and that snaps Amelia out of her "yeah" phase.

"Not since breakfast."

Hayseed looks sad. What the hell does she think Amelia does all day that she has time to just go and see Laura?

"I just…I had a question for her."

Amelia raises an eyebrow because most girls avoid Laura with a ten-foot pole outside of breakfast. "She's all right for conversations," they say. "But you wouldn't want her for a bridesmaid."

She wouldn't want Laura for a bridesmaid either.

"If I see her, I'll tell her you're looking?"

Judy nods and thanks Amelia "soooo much," and by the time Amelia pushes her way into her room, she's ready for bed—brandy and date be damned.

"Is she gone?"

Never mind. Sleep is for idiots.

Laura's sitting at her table, drink already poured. She's got on a black and purple silk robe and those red lips of hers are poised to smile.

"So, you say we're friends, and then you just sneak into my place?"

"To avoid that." Glass in hand, she points at the door.

"Way to jump on the grenade, soldier."

"Oh Amelia, I'd always jump on a grenade for you. Unfortunately, she's more like an atom bomb."

Amelia pops her shoes off and groans in relief because it's her own damn apartment. "A real cheerful one."

"How does she smile so much?"

"Right?" She starts unbuttoning her dress as she hip checks her closet open. "You'd think her cheeks would hurt."

As she sips her brandy, Laura goes quiet, and after Amelia's out of her uniform and into her dressing gown, she turns to find Laura staring straight ahead with her jaw as rigid as a Mount Rushmore president.

"So you gonna tell me how you dodged that atom bomb? Because I'm pretty sure my door was locked."

Laura blushes and drinks her brandy.

Amelia notices the breeze coming through her open window.

"You didn't climb through there did you?"

"She knocked. Multiple times."

"So you figured a two-story drop was worth the chance to escape." Normal people don't do that.

Laura shakes the brandy bottle. "The promised company helped."

Amelia drops into the chair opposite and accepts the proffered drink. She's always been a sucker for sincere flattery. Even when it's meant to distract her. "That's about the nicest thing anyone's said to me."

Laura brightens.

"This week."

The way Laura deflates makes Amelia feel a little better. She knows it isn't Laura's fault she's a high class prostitute getting banged around by guys with more money than goodness in 'em, but Amelia's day's been rotten and teasing Laura helps a little.

She's not proud of it.

She drinks too much for one gulp.

Really not proud of it.

Some of the brandy hits the wrong pipe and she coughs. Laura leans forward like she's gonna pat her on the back, and Amelia has to hold up her hand to ward her off.

Laura smirks. "Thought you Italians could handle your liquor."

"Maybe, but half of me's teetotaler Puerto Rican. Besides, you try routing it down the wrong pipe." She wheezes.

"No, I'm fine sending it down the right one, thanks." To illustrate Laura sips her brandy, and Amelia tries not to watch the way her throat undulates when she does.

"And you're really half Puerto Rican?"

"What? You think I just have an especially nice tan?"

Laura shrugs, and Amelia leans back so she can appraise her own face in the mirror. It's hanging on the closet door, clear on the other side of the apartment, but it still gives a good image. She maybe missed out on some of her dad's swarthier coloring—but her hair's dark enough and her skin's got enough of olive in it that nice places would turn their nose up at her. Least she dodged her dad's hairy bullet.

Something her sister can't say. Woman has had to shave her mustache once a week since she was twelve.

Laura honest-to-God chuckles. "I suppose I should have guessed from a last name like Maldonado. So what made your family choose Brooklyn?"

"My dad was one fella from Puerto Rico versus a whole mess of Italians boys on my mom's side. They probably would have dragged us down to South Brooklyn if he hadn't agreed."

"You make your mother's family sound…"

Amelia looks up from her drink.

"Unsavory," Laura finishes, seemingly half-embarrassed by her own words.

There's a bad joke in there about food. Amelia just shakes her head. "Most of the family is just fine."

"Most?"

"Well, every family has a bad egg, don't they? Even the Wrights, right?"

Laura pours herself another drink. "Afraid I'm the bad egg in the Wright family." She drinks half the glass and tops it off. "Twenty-eight and," she toasts no one in particular, "shamefully unmarried."

They both drink a little more and then some more, and it's only after Amelia loses count that she notices the newspapers still laid out on her coffee table. Working as a coaster for that big ol' bottle of brandy.

Laura doesn't ask about the papers. Thank God.

Instead, she talks about work—at the factory—with a hint of a grimace she fails at hiding behind her glass when she drinks. She speaks fondly of a war Amelia never hears people speak fondly of. She sips her brandy and leans her elbows on the table, and a lot of the mystique that props her up is gone.

And it should knock the bloom right off of whatever rose Amelia's carrying for her, but it doesn't.

So, she gives them some space by rising from the table and flopping onto the bed.

"You didn't spill a drop," Laura observes. She's twisted in the chair so she's facing Amelia, and Amelia's mouth is dry and other parts of her are wet. Brandy with Laura Wright after a long day was a *bad* idea.

"That's nothing. Give me six plates and a pot of coffee and then you'll really see a show."

Laura goes cipher on her again. Face perfectly still, and only her eyes moving. Focused. Piercing. Like they could see everything. "This one's good enough."

She wonders if maybe that *isn't* Laura's cipher face. Maybe it's another kind of face. Maybe she's schooling bad thoughts too.

She chews on her lip.

Laura's eyes are quick, but Amelia still sees the way they dart to her mouth and back again.

She scoots over on the bed.

Laura makes it onto the bed too. Eventually. Amelia doesn't know how long it takes because she's not about to glance at the clock. That's how spells are broken. And whatever's happening between them is a spell. Glossy and muted like a love scene in a movie.

The brandy makes it to the bed, too, and Amelia sets it on her bedside table. "Never get liquor on the sheets," she explains. "Edith's got a nose like a bloodhound."

"Just for liquor?"

She ticks them off with her fingers. "Liquor, cigarettes, reefer, hot dogs, cats, actual dogs, a ferret—I'm still not clear on how that got in—and m—"

"Men." Laura finishes Amelia's sentence with a grin. It's the closest to a giggle she's ever seen her.

"She can smell a guy even when he's on the street. One time, a girl wore her boyfriend's coat up the stairs and ol' Edith came this close to tackling her." She makes a tiny space between her thumb and finger and holds it up for Laura's amused inspection.

Laura's fingertips brush the inside of Amelia's wrist as she pushes her hand away. She's still laughing. "And the ferret? How on earth did she smell it?"

"No one knows! My theory is she's got fancy training during the war. Super soldier nose."

"Oh, they just issue those, do they?"

Because she's had one too many, she grabs Laura's nose and wiggles it gently. "You tell me."

That gets another laugh and a playful hand slap. Then Laura reaches over her to pour more brandy, and Amelia catches a glimpse of all those things she's been trying real hard not to think about. She pointedly focuses on Laura's back. The play of muscles under that silk robe. She tries not to think about the eyeful she just got. Tries not to think about how things could be real easy.

Laura's laughing as she's pouring her brandy. Her back shaking with all that mirth.

She starts to right herself, and the laughter stops.

Time stops.

It doesn't really. She's pretty sure she can hear the tick tick tick of her clock and cars on the streets and Hayseed warbling down the hall in her room.

But on the bed. In the precise confines of that mattress and frame. Time stops.

Amelia doesn't breathe because that'll kick time back into gear. Laura doesn't either.

They're just inches from each other. Face to face. Laura's knee is pressed against Amelia's thigh. A blaze of heat right there at the point of contact. Like a red-hot fire poker. Amelia can't ignore her.

She's just too close. Too there. Too much.

Amelia's breath hitches in her throat, and Laura's all cipher again. A code Amelia just wants to read and understand. She wants to know what Laura means when her eyes dart to Amelia's lips. Wants to understand why she stops breathing too. Why she goes so still. Why her face doesn't betray any of the feelings Amelia desperately needs her to return.

Amelia just wants to know why time stops when they're both so close.

Laura supplies the answer. Not with words.

Amelia can hear the clatter of Laura's glass settling onto the table and she looks toward it—the noise a distraction from the heavy moment sitting between them.

But Laura's hand on her chin stops her.

And her lips on Amelia's are all the answers she's needed.

A hand slips into her hair, and catches on a pin, then stills.

Laura's ardent.

Passionate.

Fervent.

Laura Wright kisses her, and words Amelia barely remembers reading in high school are flooding through her head. Screw being an actor and screw being good. She could be a writer like Hemingway if Laura keeps kissing her.

Nails scrape against her scalp and when she gasps, Laura's tongue slips into her mouth. Her fingers scratch at the smooth fabric of Laura's robe. Her finger tips rough in comparison. Her hands climb from the swell of Laura's hip, to the curve of her waist. And across the bulky bandages still wrapped around Laura's middle.

Just like that, time starts back up again. The hands of the clock grind forward with a pained gasp from Laura. Amelia pulls back and is pretty sure she'll never get the image of Laura's smudged lipstick and bruised lips out of her head.

Now Amelia's got the key to her cipher. Can read Laura clear as day. She's confused. Her breath is hot and sour with brandy. "Amelia."

She squeezes Laura's hip. It isn't the kiss. It isn't Laura. And it isn't because they've got no future being like they are. It's bandages still tight around Laura's ribs. It's the shadow of the cut behind her ear. It's her own cousin with a cracked skull.

Amelia swallows. "When you came to the diner half passed out, where were you coming from?"

Laura's not quite as breathless anymore. "Work."

Amelia wants to rub small circles with her thumb and never forget how Laura's body is both hard and soft. "What kind of work?"

And now she's all hard. She's a wolf with teeth and she's far too close. "Why are you so determined to find out?"

"Why are you so determined to hide?"

"Don't." She says it like a command. Like she's said it before and people listened.

"Laura, I like you, but any way you look at us, this is gonna hurt. And right now—" Laura's up and off the bed abruptly, so all Amelia's words can do is chase after her. "Right now, I'm thinkin' you're gonna kill me."

Laura's whole body sinks when she sighs. "I never wanted to kill you, Amelia." Then she's out the door. It doesn't even slam. Just clicks shut as if they were in there playing bridge.

Amelia cleans up the glasses and hides the brandy away.

She doesn't think about what Laura said. Not because it hurts. As soon as Laura kissed her, she knew it was all gonna hurt.

It was the way she said it—that she never wanted to kill her. She said it like she was sorry. Not for what she'd done, but what she was going to do.

CHAPTER 4

AMELIA DOESN'T DREAM OF KISSING Laura. Even a little bit.

Okay, that's a lie.

She doesn't dream of Laura, because, point in fact, she doesn't dream. Because she doesn't sleep. She tries, of course, but then she starts running over the conversation and what might have been a veiled threat. Even though she really, really wants to sleep, she just twists around under the covers until the sun's up in the sky and pale light streams through the window.

The sky's a gray haze with a little yellow because there's a great big sun behind it. But mainly it's gray. And the city's gray, too. It's as depressing as walking through the sea of fellows in the same suits and hats on the way to the train.

It stays gray all day. It brings down the mood of the folks who come in asking for a cup of coffee or a ham and cheese sandwich.

Amelia, being the middle kid between two brothers who always had to step between fights and sooth ruffled boy feathers, just smiles harder. Her cheeks hurt by the end of the day, and that makes her think of her and Laura talking about Hayseed. And that makes the rest of her hurt because Laura Wright's slit a hole in Amelia's skin and crawled inside. She's pretty sure there's no way she's gonna get her out.

Traveling to Brooklyn after work is more of an ordeal than usual. The train's backed up and decides to skip her stop, which sends her twenty minutes and one bus ride out of her way. When she finally steps onto the narrow, tree-lined street her uncle lives on, the sun's well past set and most folks have moved off their stoops to warm up inside. A couple of houses are glowing with friendliness, and she can see families gathering around eating warm dinners.

Amelia's stomach wishes she was there for a warm dinner.

But nope. Instead, her uncle's sitting on the bench in his front garden. The whole neighborhood is built up in blocky brownstones with big front gardens that stretch out toward the street. A lot of 'em have actual gardens—full of food for eating.

Her uncle just has a big tree and lots of flowers and prickly bushes you wouldn't want to fall in. When it's sunny out, he totters around with a watering can and pretends to be older and more senile than he is.

But now he's just sitting on his bench, reading one of his mystery books. He idolizes the guys in them. Fellas like Nick Charles and Sam Spade. Smart guys. Good guys. But nasty when they have to be. Bashing heads in and keeping the peace through violence there in South Brooklyn. Her uncle probably thinks he's just like those guys.

She peers at the spine when she's close enough. It's about as far from hard-boiled, boy fiction as it can be. "Machiavelli," she says, her nose wrinkling. "Really? Was *I Want Everyone to Think I'm Evil Incarnate* checked out of the library or something?"

He chuckles, and it's supposed to be warm, but it chills her through. She pulls her light coat tighter around herself.

"Running your mouth is what always gets you into trouble, Amelia." He licks his thumb and turns the page. Never looks at her. She's not *worth* it. Not yet. Not to him.

She's gotta earn his respect.

It rankles her. She shifts on her heels, juts out her jaw, and sucks on her front teeth.

"You should sit."

"I'm fine standing."

"After all day in that diner? No, baby doll. Sit."

She takes the seat next to him and watches him read by the light of the street lamp.

"There a reason—"

He cuts her off just by lifting his hand. Still doesn't look at her. So she stares at him hard. He's got big knuckles, thick with arthritis and fleshy fingers that end in neatly trimmed nails. He used to come over, listen to the radio with the whole family, and clip and file them. Real neat like. Clip and file.

"How's your brother?"

He only means one brother, because the other two still live in the city and probably see him during big family dinners on Sunday. "Happy in Nebraska," she says. "He's got a little garage he runs. Wants my ma to come out and visit."

"Not you?"

She studies the flowers he's tended to since his wife died. Studying them is better than socking her uncle in the mouth.

"What about acting? You still acting, Amelia?"

One of her hands squeezes the strap of her purse tight and the other digs into her thigh.

He's not looking at her yet, but his tone is needling. "Still playing pretend?"

She stands jerkily. "Weeeeell, this was real fun. My cousin ever wakes up, you tell him I said hi."

Her uncle still hasn't looked up. "Why'd you call about your cousin?"

It's actual curiosity. Which isn't something her uncle tends toward. And he's playing like he doesn't care, but he'd never have asked if he didn't. She sits back down. "I was worried."

He harrumphs. "We both know how you feel about him. About all of 'em."

"Yeah. I love the big ape. Him, late trains, and enemas. My favorite things."

It's a pretty coarse thing to say, and if her dad were still alive, he would have thumped her with that big gold family ring of his.

Her uncle just glares with those narrow eyes. Like chips of dark glass. "I get the feeling it wasn't for him. Or even you."

"You know my ma. Always worried about the nephew she can't stand."

It rolls off him like water in a hot pan. "See, I get the feeling you're doing this for *her*." Her uncle knows Amelia. Knows things about her the rest of the family can't. So he can take something simple like a pronoun and twist it into something... nasty.

She's proud of herself. She doesn't squeak or anything. Doesn't even bulge her eyes a little. Instead she tilts her head back and hopes she looks defiant. "You gonna keep dancing like Fred or you gonna tell me who exactly you think I'm doing this for."

"That woman. The one who cracked my son's skull nearly in two and got Jimmy Andronico so scared, no one's seen him since."

Jimmy Andronico. Of course. The other guy messing with Laura that night has to be the only guy in the whole wide world to ever get a hand up Amelia's skirt. Not for the first time, she's proud of Laura.

But she snorts. "You really think I'd know a broad like that?"

He's still staring.

"You gotta be kidding."

"You show up out of the blue asking questions. And I know the kind of friends you keep Amelia. Real funny girls."

Real funny girls. Queer even. Like her. She's got her jaw clinched so tight she might crack a tooth.

Her uncle leans in. Tobacco on his breath. "Who is she?"

How can she say when she doesn't even know? "I got no idea, Vince. But I do gotta wonder why my cousin and Jimmy are running around with broads who aren't their wives."

He's got a gaze like one of them sphinxes in Egypt. Trying to read her behind those little glasses. But Vince Pedrotti hasn't been able to lay her bare in years, and he's not gonna get back in the habit with a few intimations and lousy questions.

"Whatever—whoever—you're flirting with," his jaw barely moves as he speaks, "you'd be wise to give it a rest. You're no sixteen-year-old girl with a dad down in the garage to protect you."

"And you're not the big, bad bossman you used to be. So save the threats for someone who gives a hoot."

She gets up and heads for the gate, but her uncle calls after her, all cool like, "What makes you think I'm the one doing the threatening, baby doll? You're trying to force your way into a party you got no invitation for. Maybe you ought to stick to the wall on this dance."

"Yeah, well, I've never been a wallflower."

The gate groans like an old man as she slams it closed with her heel. At the far end of the street a '39 Oldsmobile rounds the corner and brakes to a noisy stop. She can't see who's driving. But she hears them drop into reverse and watches the headlights wink out.

It's not fear like snow down her back, because Amelia's no lily liver. But it's definitely something, and blood pounds like a drum in her ears.

Her uncle laughs, and when she turns real quick to look at him, his lips are curved up in a sick joke of a smile. "Better be careful, Amelia. I'm thinking you don't know all the steps to this number."

His laughter follows her all the way back to the train.

Thankfully, the '39 Oldsmobile does not.

She fidgets when they go under the East River.

Amelia'd had a plan. Made from well-reasoned assumptions. And now her uncle's gone and ripped the rug out from under her. Laid her out on her ass with nothing but a couple of words.

Maybe Laura isn't some down on her luck girl in need of a hero. Maybe she's the predator instead of the prey. Which doesn't account for that no good Tall, Dark, and French. Unless he's in on it. Her getaway driver for murders.

But murderers don't just live in little all-women hotels. They don't ingratiate themselves into Amelia's life.

Whatever Laura is she isn't the evil darkening Vince Pedrotti's doorstep.

She can't be.

Amelia gets off a stop early and slips into a diner to use their phonebook. She almost tries Jimmy's house first, but the ball and chain strapped to his ankle, Doris LaManna Andronico, has hated Amelia since second grade when they kissed. Amelia said it was nice. Doris said it was gross and shoved her in the gravel.

Okay, so maybe Amelia hated Doris for that one.

But Doris definitely hated Amelia after she briefly stole Jimmy away to get back at Doris for telling everyone she was secretly a boy.

Just because a gal likes kissing other gals, doesn't mean she's a boy. Just means she's got tastes. Predilections.

Anyways. Doris LaManna Andronico is a bitch. Iris Andronico, Jimmy's dear old mom, is not. A drunk, yes. Bitch, no.

And besides, she loves Amelia. Says she was "real good" for her boy.

She calls and speaks brightly and says she'd "just love to talk to Jimmy."

Iris hems and haws. "Haven't seen him in days," she says. "I'm starting to get worried."

Amelia says she "knows." Says it in that way only folks from the neighborhood can say it. Because some boys work in garages and others work on the docks, and some boys slick their hair back and wear nice suits and do very, very bad things.

All she does is say she'd like to talk to Jimmy. If he calls. She's "worried too." She just "wants to help."

"You're such a good girl." Iris sniffs. "Why couldn't you have stayed with Jimmy? You were so good together."

She doesn't have the heart to tell her they dated for two months, and it was the most boring and awkward two months of her life. Doesn't have the heart to tell her about birds and bees and girls who like girls.

"I wonder, too," she softly lies.

She gets to the Sebastian five minutes before curfew. Same time as Laura, who steps out of a private car looking glamorous and put together and remarkably bruise free.

Then she sees Amelia.

She falters for half a second. "Amelia." She says it all breathy, and it's enough to make Amelia want to drag her upstairs and just—just talk.

"Hot date?" Amelia asks.

"Rather frustrating actually. Confusing even." Laura cocks her head. "What about you? I thought you were done early today."

"Saw a movie. Took a walk. Enjoyed the fog."

Laura laughs lightly. "What'd you see? Anything good?"

"I thought about seeing that new flick, Gilda? You know the one about the gorgeous broad twisting an idiot up in knots? Think there's some Nazis in it, too."

Laura misses a step, but is smooth as silk in her recovery. "H-how was it?"

She shrugs. "Don't know. Saw Harvey Girls again instead. It's a garbage flick, but it's kind of nice to watch someone like Judy Garland in something so miserable." She reaches the door before Laura and turns on her heel. "We all gotta do bad things sometimes, right?"

Laura's mouth works and nothing comes out.

So Amelia smiles softly, because it's like Laura's always got something to say, even when she doesn't say it.

"See ya later."

CHAPTER 5

THE NEXT DAY IS THE best day. Ever. In Amelia Maldonado's life. That audition she bombed so bad they call it London? She gets a callback.

"Next week," they say. "Wear red."

She whoops.

Maybe she hollers a little. She vibrates all through her afternoon shift and doesn't even falter in that pathetically sad little way when she remembers she can't tell Laura all about it and watch her tight smile.

Laura.

There's the sour note on a very good day.

Laura. Who supposedly cracked her cousin's skull. Laura. Who has her uncle, a man who never runs scared, nervous. Laura. Who's maybe wrapped up in something more than prostitution. Laura. Who kissed her like it was V-J Day.

Laura.

As golden a day as it is—and it *is* golden—Amelia still sighs a lot. And every time, it's because of stupid Laura Wright.

The biggest sigh comes when Laura walks through the door. She looks at Amelia, then looks away. And then she comes and sits at the empty counter.

Laura studies Amelia as she works. Eyes hot and focused. Lips pulled tightly together. Laura has a habit of sittin' rigid. That's her armor. Amelia gets it. She wears armor too. All the girls do. Sass talk or smiles or golly gee whizzes or all of the above. There's a way the world is always gonna look at a girl who's trying to make it without a fella. So, on the armor goes, first thing in the morning. Usually as the last curler falls out of the hair and that last bit of lipstick is applied.

Laura's armor feels like real armor though, as if she needs a bulwark between her and the rest of the world. It's probably what makes her so addictive. 'Cause when Amelia gets glimpses of what's behind those sharp eyes, sharp tongue, and straight back, she's utterly enchanted.

Enamored.

She wordlessly gives Laura her coffee and puts in her usual order. She doesn't ignore Laura. She's not a baby.

She just...Well, the point is, she's not real sure how to act. It's not every day she kisses a girl, sort of fights with her, and then calls her an apocalypse.

Laura breaks the silence with a bark of laughter that's soft enough not to bring the whole diner's attention down on their heads.

"We're a disaster."

She's not wrong. Amelia smiles. "How's the factory?" It's part apology, part accusation.

A shrug. "How's the diner?" That sounds a whole lot more like an accusation.

Her knuckles go white on the handle of the coffee pot. "Busy."

Laura nods, and Amelia isn't really sure what's going on. There's enough levels to their conversation that it feels heady—like leaning off the Empire State Building.

"I got a call back," she says abruptly.

Real abruptly, judging by Laura's startled look. Then she looks confused. Finally, she smiles. And not that brittle fake one.

It's the real one.

"That's wonderful, Amelia."

"Week from today."

"A nice role?"

"A big one. I'm telling you, Laura. I get this one, and in ten years, Cary Grant's giving me an Oscar."

"Where's the show? I'll make a point to get tickets."

"You know, if I'm in it, I can just comp 'em. That's gotta be a perk, right? Because it sure isn't the pay. Not careful, I'll have a Tony and still be minding these counters."

"Tips should improve."

She's gonna laugh. She really is. It's a funny joke, and it deserves a laugh. And Laura's being easy again, and that *always* invites happy little bubbly feelings. So she grins and her mouth falls open—but then she can't laugh. Because the glass doors spin and deposit Jimmy Andronico in her diner.

Laura notices her joke isn't getting the results it should. She barely glances back at Jimmy. Just out the corner of her eye without moving any other part of her. "Friend?"

"Sure."

Amelia crosses the room in quick strides and ushers Jimmy over to a booth.

"Jimmy," she says brightly. Her hand latches onto his bicep, and she squeezes it tight. "What the heck are you doing here," she asks in a hurried whisper.

"You called my ma—" His reply is cut short by her shoving him into the booth.

Laura sits at the counter and actually eats her sandwich. Taking those big bulging bites that are so at odds with that classy way of talking she's got. If she recognizes Jimmy, she's the one that ought to be getting the Oscar from Cary Grant.

Amelia smiles brightly and whips out her pad. "What can I get ya, honey?"

"I don't really have any—"

"Turkey plate and a cup of coffee," she says loudly. "Can do! Anything el—"

"Look, Amelia, you're the one calling my—"

"Okay! I'll be right back with that coffee."

She rips the order off the pad as she walks. Tries not to be too stiff. Laura has a newspaper out and is perusing it with one hand while holding her sandwich with the other. She watches Amelia as she walks by. Not quite that cipher look of hers, because Amelia is pretty sure this one is her "I want you naked and panting now" look.

She passes Jimmy's ticket off to the cook and shoots Laura something kind of like an apology as she snags the coffee pot and a cup. "Be right back," she says.

Laura waves her off. "No rush," she says—mouth still loaded for bear with ham and cheese.

Back at the booth, Jimmy's fidgety. He's also chalky and haggard and basically looking like a soldier straight out of a POW camp.

"When I called your mom," she says out the corner of her mouth, "I didn't think you were gonna actually show up at my work."

"Seemed more polite than coming to your hotel."

Her eyebrow hops up all on its own. "For not talking to me in ten years, you know an awful lot about me."

55

He's kinda sweet when he looks up at her and smiles. "Church." Like that explains everything.

Okay, it does actually explain everything.

"Doris must love that."

He looks down at his coffee. "Nope." How this guy got into the line of work he's in, Amelia doesn't know. He's about as guileless as her three-year-old niece.

Across the diner, a James Cagney wannabe shouts, "Hey sweetheart, you got other customers, you know!"

At the counter, Laura stops eating her sandwich to whip around and glare. She's surprised the guy doesn't completely combust by the time she gets to him.

She finishes with Cagney, pours coffee for two more tables, nods at Laura again and then returns to Jimmy. He eats his turkey plate like a man that's been denied. There's lots of gross lip smacking and that real annoying noise a person makes in the back of their throat when he's trying to breathe and eat at once.

Even though her mom's in her head telling her to be more gracious, Amelia doesn't bother hiding the disgust on her face.

"You not looking too good, Jimmy. Rough racket?"

He glances up with hard eyes. "Yeah… I need you to give your uncle a message. I'm out."

"You think I'm talking to him?"

"More like working for him." He glances around. "Arranging things through you is real smart of him. Out in the open. Neutral. Like Sweden."

"Switzerland." She shakes her head. "And I don't work for my uncle."

"Then why're you looking for me?"

"Because my cousin—"

He snorts into his turkey and gravy.

"I could like my cousin." She couldn't. But she's still gonna be defensive about it.

Jimmy looks at her the exact way a person's allowed to after he gets his hand up your dress.

"Curiosity," she says succinctly.

He believes that one about as much as she does.

"Look," she sighs. "I know you all were running girls and apparently you bit off more than you could chew. All I want to know is what happened that night."

That goes as far as a dollar at the tracks. Jimmy just looks confused.

"The woman," she says slowly. Like maybe that'll explain everything.

And maybe it does.

Just saying it makes Jimmy's face contort. He goes paler than he already was—so he's basically the color of the plate he's eating off of—and he gets kind of angry too. Around his eyes a whole lot of emotions are hitting the guy at once, and she's worried he's gonna have a fit and go face down into the brown gravy.

"Your mom know about you?" It comes out as kind of a sneer.

She blinks.

Some stuff she's obligated to respond to, but this stuff? Folks in the neighborhood and the stuff they might say about her? *That* she's just gonna sit on. She learned a long time ago that fighting that kind of stupidity is sort of like beating your head against a windshield to get out of a car. It might work, but it sure is gonna hurt. And there'll be scars for years.

Amelia ignores the question. Pours him more coffee. "Did you see her?"

He studies her. Is careful with his words—even though venom laces them like a blade in an adventure picture. "Yeah, I saw her."

"She really crack my cousin's skull?"

He snorts. "His and six other guys."

She stops pouring. Jimmy's too busy slurping up coffee and wolfing down turkey to notice the way her hand is shaking.

"Whatever you're thinking, Amelia, it wasn't girls we were running. Your uncle? He's got friends back in Italy that needed something moved. Idea was we'd do the moving. All we had to do was wait in the bar 'til the folks came around. Exchange it for cash. Easy money."

Amelia works real hard not to look back at Laura—who may not be the high-class girl Amelia's been thinking she's got to save.

"How easy?"

"Grand per fellow in the room. More for your uncle and his pals overseas."

She takes her lord and savior, Jesus Christ's, name in vain. "Jesus Jimmy." A few people look up. She ducks down and speaks quickly. "There were seven of you in the room. That's at least seven thousand dollars."

"Shoulda known it was too good to be true. But we figured if there was trouble, we'd see it. Guys with guns you know? But it wasn't no guy or gun."

"A dame." A dame who may or may not be sitting on a stool ten feet away.

"She came in all breathy. Just sighing and acting cute. So Frankie, Frankie himself takes her back for a 'tour.'" Jimmy can only manage the air quotes with one hand. "It's the rest of us in the front. Waiting on the pickup. Then there's this noise. Like a yelp, and we run in there because it's not a happy yelp. We find her with her knee halfway up his..." he motions down at his pants, "and her fingers up his nose, and she's pulling like she's gonna just rip it off."

"Jesus." That's all she can say, because her brains still working to catch up.

"Then smack and pow. By the end of it, your cousin and I are the only ones standing."

"You fight her?"

He shakes his head. "We ran. She chased. Cousin got cracked with a pool cue."

"How'd you get away?"

He coughs and sort of folds to one side. "Didn't. Stabbed me through with the same cue. But then the cops were coming one way and the folks for the pickup come the other. I wasn't about to stick around."

She peeks around his jacket and blanches. There's blood. Old and new. A lot of it. Enough to give her flashes of unpleasant memories—she shakes her head. Nope. She's not gonna go down a rabbit hole.

Instead, she kneels by him and puts a hand on his shoulder. It's narrow and bony against her palm. "You gotta see a doctor."

He shakes his head. "Can't. They're watching."

"Who? My uncle? Jimmy, my uncle's just gonna be glad you're alive."

"I don't think so."

"Why not?"

All the food and coffee's given him energy and turned him feverish. His eyes are wide. "I took what he was selling, Amelia. I accidentally stole from your uncle."

Shit.

"And his clients."

Double shit.

"And whoever he was selling to."

Triple. Quadruple.

"And her."

Just shit.

Laura's still at the counter eating. Still unassuming. Still the Laura she knew *before* Jimmy walked through the revolving door.

She bites her lip. Because, if she's gonna be honest, she's confused. And out of her depth. And confused.

Jimmy was supposed to come in all puffed up and ready to lie. Then she was supposed to tell him to drop the act, lay off the prostitutes, and spill the name of the pimp.

He wasn't supposed to come in half dead and hunted.

She straightens up again and glances back at Laura.

It's just a moment. One little instance. She looks past the broad line of Laura's shoulders and catches her reflection in the chrome blender just beyond.

Who she makes eye contact with *isn't* that sweet distant woman she kissed, the one she has been half killing herself trying to help.

It's something sharp and savage and familiar.

She's so shocked, she bumps into the table. Flatware clatters noisily and half the automat stops briefly to stare.

Laura whips around to look at her all inscrutable like.

Amelia would like to think Laura's looking shocked and sorry. Only she's still seeing that other face—that reflection.

"Jimmy," she doesn't take her eyes off Laura, still frozen on her stool. "You need to leave. Now."

She's not sure if he sees Laura at the counter. He must. "You'll be okay?"

She hasn't taken her eyes off Laura.

His clothes rustle as he stands, and he squeezes her hand and presses wet, cold lips to her cheek before fleeing. "Thanks, Amelia."

Across the room, Laura's gone cool. All that posh, upper-crust reserve freezes her into an ice sculpture.

So Amelia crosses the room, steps measured. Her heels sound too loud against the linoleum. And she still doesn't take her eyes off Laura. She can't.

"So he is a friend," Laura finally says when they're face to face with just the counter between them.

"Yeah. Lookin' like the only one I got in the joint."

"I'm not entirely clear," Laura is conversational, "what your game is, Amelia Maldonado."

She can be conversational, too. So she leans on the counter. "You know? The same thing's been crossing my mind."

That gets her one raised eyebrow.

Then Laura's sipping her drink and purposely taking her eyes off Amelia. "I suppose you could lay your cards on the table. Explain yourself."

"How 'bout you try first. Because I'm not the one that's gotta explain a pool cue between a fella's ribs."

"Well, that's a bit complicated."

"Only because you make it that way."

There's a little crack in Laura's armor. For a half second, she gets an addictive glimpse of what's going on beneath.

And Amelia thinks *if* she can just snag the right words, she can use them like a dagger. Slide right in through the crack and take the whole mess down.

But tires screech and horns blare and metal crunches outside. Like just about everyone else, they both rush to the window to gawk.

Amelia sees a familiar shock of black hair at the center of the mess of cars. She runs through the revolving door and ignores Laura calling after her.

She runs, and even though she and God are on the outs, she throws up a little prayer.

Which is worthless. There's no prayer that's gonna help Jimmy Andronico now. Not when he's crushed between two cars and his blood is bright like paint on the street.

Her heel catches on a crack in the pavement and she dips. Then she rights herself. Stumbles through the crowd to be beside him. Ignores the men telling her to come away.

"You shouldn't see this," they say. Like she's never seen something so awful before.

Jimmy twitches, there's blood on his lips, and his eyes flutter open and closed. She tries to say something, but she's not real sure what to say to a dying man.

Jimmy doesn't know what to say either. But he reaches for her. Holds her hand tight in his. It's sticky and going cold.

Then whatever makes a fella a fella just flickers out of Jimmy. All that's left is some flesh pressed between two cars.

She lets the crowd pull her back. Glances down at the hard piece of metal Jimmy put in her hand before he died.

A roll of film.

A roll of film at least six fellas are dead over.

A roll of film Laura's maybe killed for.

She spins around.

Laura's standing there. Just out of arm's reach.

She could be stricken.

Could be satisfied.

Could be angry.

Amelia can't tell.

They stare at each other until the crowd swells around them and Laura vanishes into it.

Then all Amelia can do is think.

About how Laura had said she didn't want to kill her.

She kind of thought that Laura was being a romantic idiot when she said it. Hoped as much too.

But now?

Now, she's pretty sure she just painted a target on her back, and Laura's off to set her sights.

CHAPTER 6

THE COPS DON'T ASK A lot of questions of the crowd, or of Amelia, who now has a bloody film canister shoved into her dress pocket. They stare at Jimmy's body. One says "accident," and another nods.

Accident.

Amelia shivers.

Jimmy's dead, and it isn't an accident.

She's confused and scared and things are spinning all wrong, but she knows an accident. Especially a car accident. And this one reeks of purpose.

"He stumbled out in front of me," one driver says.

"Just out of nowhere," the other says.

She watches that one. He talks about seeing a gorgeous dame on the street. Red hair. Sweet smile. Great legs. He was distracted.

"Accident" Amelia's ass.

She's jittery through the end of service and doesn't even blink when she realizes neither Jimmy nor Laura paid and it's gotta come out of her own pocket.

Things are spinning.

The film is burning a hole in her pocket.

She can't sit on the train home. She bounces too much, and people start avoiding her bench. So, she stands close to the door and stares out the window at dark tunnels.

Jimmy's squished like a tomato, and Amelia can't stop feeling like she had a hand in it. Like she really did set him up.

Only she can't figure who has folded her into this. Her uncle's a snake if there ever was one. But Laura beat a whole room of men senseless and came away with nothing but a cut head, some bruised ribs and a bad lie.

Amelia is spinning and spinning and spinning 'round these lies. So much so that she doesn't realize the power in the hotel is out until she's in her room and flipping a worthless switch. That explains why so many girls are milling about outside of their rooms and so many of their boys are downstairs cuddling and comforting them like the war is back on.

She changes out of her uniform and slips on a different pair of shoes, figuring she'll look up an old friend who knows a thing or two about pictures. Maybe she can get the roll developed. Figure out who all is involved and...

Figure something out.

Then she notices there's a breeze coming through a window she never leaves open and was definitely closed when she walked in.

Nothing's spinning any more. It's crystal clear.

Hands snake around her waist and over her mouth and pull her back like a python. Before she can scream, she smells Laura's perfume and feels her hot breath in her ear. Laura's not killing her. There's no knife or quick jerk of her neck. Just Laura holding her close and breathing hard.

And there's no talking because, as she tries to twist around and look at Laura, Laura's looking elsewhere. A hand comes off her mouth and points at the door.

The knob twitches.

Laura drags her farther into the shadows of an already dark room. Her chest is heaving against Amelia's back, her breath is hot puffs on her neck. If someone wasn't trying to break into Amelia's apartment, and she wasn't confused as to how Laura can move quiet as a mouse, she'd be having a whole mess of other more pleasant thoughts.

The fingers at her waist dig in, pulling her closer. Pressing her up against Laura like cellophane. She shudders and Laura's grip loosens just barely. Enough so that her thumb can play across Amelia's stomach.

Ah jeeze. She's screwed.

Laura's other hand brushes Amelia's arm as she reaches back toward herself, and Amelia has to close her eyes because she's having thoughts when it really isn't the time or place.

When she opens them again, she sees the gun.

Laura's not like the boys from her neighborhood. The gun doesn't wobble, she holds it steady. Barrel pointed toward that door.

It opens silently. And there's no light to leak in because the electricity is all out, and now Amelia's got an idea as to why.

A figure all in black moves through the darkness, melding with the shadows they're all lurking in.

Laura's fingers dig into Amelia's belly.

Then the world explodes in flashes of light and sulphur.

A hollow *bang bang bang* that makes her ears ring and her blood roar.

Laura shoves her forward and maybe shouts, "Go!"

So Amelia goes.

Out the corner of her eye, she sees Laura charging the other person and sees the flash of another gun firing.

The other one's fast, like a featherweight. But Laura's a goddamned freight train.

In the hall, girls are screaming and scrambling in chaos. The lights out had everyone on edge anyway, and now the gunshots have sent them screeching over it.

She pushes through and jogs down the stairs and out onto the street. She's breathing fast, and her blood is up like she's sixteen again.

A couple of guys are outside, leaning against a car and looking too neat and businesslike to be boys waiting on a couple of girls inside. They perk up when they notice her.

Which... well, whatever's going on, guys marching toward her cannot be good. She starts walking the other way, a hitch in her step. She resists the urge to all out run.

Then Laura is by her side, a little breathless, her arm snakes around Amelia, and a great big smile is plastered on her face. "Keep walking," she says without moving her lips. "And don't look back."

So she keeps walking. Their heels clack on the sidewalk.

And she tries real hard not to look back.

"Laura," she says real low.

Laura squeezes her arm. "It's all right." Her head is held high as if she means it.

"I got a feeling you know more than me right now."

A ghost of a smile graces those full red lips of hers. "I have a feeling you're right."

"Care to share?"

Her jaw sets. "When you're safe."

"They still following us?"

"They are. In a moment we're going to go into an alley. There's a car. We should get in it."

Amelia must tense up, because Laura's soothing her with that thumb of hers. The one moving in gentle circles to the left of her spine.

"It's all right, Amelia. I'll do everything in my power to keep you safe."

"Promise?"

She feels Laura's eyes on her, and oh, how they burn. "Promise."

The fellas pick up their pace as Amelia and Laura round into the alley. A dark blue Cadillac, missing its plates, is sitting there, front facing out. Amelia slides into the driver's seat and then across the bench into the passenger seat as Laura pushes in.

"Just keep your head down," she urges.

"Laura where in the bleedin' heck did you get a car? You didn't—"

Laura snatches a screwdriver from under the seat and jams it into the ignition. "Borrowed it," she says with a grunt.

The car roars to life as Laura nearly floods the carburetor with gas.

"Tall, Dark, and French?"

"Excuse me?"

"This his?"

"No." She actually huffs when she says it.

The guys are standing shoulder to shoulder at the other end of the alley. The Cadillac's lights blaze on their matching dark suits and shine on their matching— "Guns!"

One of Laura's hands pushes Amelia down to the floorboard, and she drives straight for the men, not even flinching as their bullets ping off the hood and crack the windshield.

She's...Amelia sits up after the car twists onto the road and just stares at Laura. Because the streetlamps are lighting Laura like some sculpture out of Europe, and that narrow jaw, high cheekbones, and dark eyes are all resolute.

Not for the first time, just looking at Laura steals all the breath out of Amelia.

"Are you hit?" Laura asks. She takes her eyes off the road to scan Amelia.

"No, I'm fine. Laura what—"

"I thought you were with the Russians."

That's a new one.

Laura shakes her head. She's so damn earnest. Honest even. Amelia's never seen it on her. "Or some fascist faction. You were so curious, and with your uncle and cousin—" She snorts. Laura breathes in sharp through her nose. "These last two days, I was sure you were a spy sent to kill me."

"You thought I was a spy?"

Laura nods. Like she's relieved.

Like all those sort of threats she's laid at Amelia's feet can be forgotten.

"What changed your mind?" Amelia asks.

"The way you looked when that man died today. You can't fake that kind of shock and confusion."

Maybe, but Amelia likes to think she's a pretty good actress.

Wait. "So does that mean you're a spy?"

"An agent." Laura's voice is tight. "Former." Before Amelia can dig into that nugget of information, Laura rounds on her. "Amelia what on earth were you doing?"

Okay. Amelia doesn't often want to slap another woman upside the head—especially one she's sweet on. "Me?"

"Asking questions. Meeting with mobsters. Taking highly sensitive information from a dead man. This isn't some thriller you pay a dime to see."

"No shit, Sherlock. Figured that out when my only ever boyfriend got smashed like catsup today." All that red's never gonna leave her head.

Laura glances away and looks sorry. "I...I had no idea you were so close."

"Yeah, I mean I only dated him to get back at this girl." Something in her eyes is burning, and she has to dig the heels of her hands in to soothe it. She sniffs. "So, Miss Former Agent. You gonna tell me what's going on?"

"That war we all fought? It never ended."

Well, that's succinct.

"And what? I stumbled into the next D-Day?"

Another smile. Amelia really knows how to pull 'em out of her.

"In a manner of speaking. Italian communists smuggled stolen Nazi weapon plans and were planning to sell them to the Russians. Your uncle is the middle man. Though I don't think he realizes who he's dealing with."

Cute. Laura thinking her uncle doesn't know every which way of the deal that went south.

Laura shakes her head again, "I understand your family's involvement. But whatever possessed you?"

She pulls her legs up onto the bench and wraps her arms around them. Squeezing herself into an uncomfortable ball.

Because here it is.

Earlier Laura had asked for cards on the table, and now it's time for Amelia to do as much. She sucks in a breath and lets it out, watching as it fogs the window.

"It's silly."

"You nearly died for something silly?"

Amelia rests her chin on her knees. They're at Lincoln Tunnel now, and the light comes in gentle waves as they pass under each garish yellow bulb. "So there's this girl."

Laura starts to smile and then catches herself.

Amelia continues. "Comes in every day and a lot of nights. Smiles like she's seen the world end. And when she looks at me, I want to do the ending. And this one night. This one night, she comes in roughed up. You know, I've seen her roughed up before."

Laura twists the steering wheel in her bare hands, but she doesn't speak.

"But I'm a classy lady, so I don't say nothing. But this time, this time it's bad. And when I do just the teeniest bit of investigating, I find the folks who did the roughin' are my own idiot family. I think that maybe, possibly, I can see to it she's not getting roughed up anymore. I felt obliged."

"Obliged?"

She sighs. It's gonna sound stupid. In the wake of spies and saving the world, she's gonna look a fool. But she's gotta say it. "To have a chat with your pimp."

Apparently, this revelation is shocking, because Laura swerves off the road and back onto it again. Gravel spits up into the undercarriage of the car and makes an awful racket. Even though they're nearly out of civilization now and there's no light to speak of, Amelia's sure she sees a blush.

"A prostitute! All this time you thought I was a prostitute?"

"Only since last week. And why are you acting so shocked?"

"I told you I work at a factory. How on earth does that lend itself to 'lady of the night'?"

"Well, how else do you explain that fella ferrying you around?"

"The obvious conclusion. Spy."

"Excuse me, Mata Hari. Besides, I don't see why you're so upset. Whores can be plenty classy. Who are the biggest tippers at church? Whores and mobsters."

Laura bristles with indignant WASPness. "I'm neither."

"Good to know."

"Thank you." She seems cranky.

They're out of the city and headed deep into Jersey. Amelia's not real sure where exactly they're aiming for, and Laura seems too annoyed for her to ask.

The silence stretches.

"Your cousin and his friends? I presume you thought they beat me in some sort of—"

"Kinky sex thing? Yeah. I was gonna tell all their wives."

"Did it never cross your mind that it all might have backfired?"

"Oh honey, I know where just about all those boys' skeletons are hidden. The worst they could have done to me was tell my mom stuff she already knows."

More silence. Laura chews on Amelia's words like they're some hearty bread.

"Is she all right with it?" She glances at her. "With you?"

That big pit that wells up when folks talk about Amelia's predilections doesn't show up this time. Amelia stares back. "What do you think?"

"But you still have a relationship?"

"Denial. Hurts like hell but gets me invited to Sunday dinners."

Laura's got nothing to say to that. Her face is all inscrutable as her brain works on things she's not gonna privy Amelia to. She just keeps driving. Darkness overtakes them the farther they go. Fewer cars. Greater distance between houses. The road lulls Amelia. And before she knows it, her eyes are closing.

Last thing she sees before sleep is Laura's profile. Hard and dangerous.

An agent, Laura called herself.

She smiles sleepily.

Amelia Maldonado's gone and fallen in love with a spy.

And who knew. It hurts just as bad as if she were a prostitute.

CHAPTER 7

THE CAR RATTLES TO A stop—accompanied by hurried French cursing. It pulls Amelia out of her sleep, and she glances at the clock on the dash. Past midnight.

Outside, the damp of the last few days has broken into a soft rain.

"Where are we?" she asks.

Laura is fiddling with the screwdriver and the gas pedal and muttering to herself. "Middle of fucking nowhere."

Amelia's eyebrow climbs halfway up her face, and while she'd like to ask if Laura kisses her mother with that mouth, instead she says, "We been driving all this time?"

"Of course. Why?—"

"Radiator, Laura. It's probably overheated." The hissing noise coming from the front end, loud enough to hear over the patter of the rain, is a dead giveaway.

Laura looks like she doesn't believe it. Then she shakes her head and gets out. She's still mumbling, and her frustration with something as simple as a broken down car has Amelia working hard not to smile.

The hood flips up, and Laura stands in the headlights, hand on hip, clearly annoyed, and making no effort to hide it.

The cool spy who drove half the night in a stolen car probably doesn't know the radiator from the carburetor.

So Amelia ignores Laura's gentle protest and gets out. "Could be gas, too. I'm betting this thing wasn't filled up when we headed outta town."

Laura blushes.

Steam's coming off the engine. Definitely overheated. "We have any water?"

Laura waves to the rain. "We've got plenty of water. It will just take a little time to collect it."

Amelia goes around to the back of the car and squats down. The gravel is already turning grimy, and it's gonna leave marks on her nice clean dress. Laura is clearly confused as to what she's doing, so she just watches, arms crossed over her chest, and the rain makes short work of her normally fastidious curls.

Bracing herself against the bumper, Amelia reaches under the car and flicks the gas tank with her knuckle.

The hollow sound faintly audible above the rain makes her wince.

Laura's not just grumpy. Now she's petulant. "We're also out of gas, aren't we?"

"Nothing but fumes."

She curses again.

Laura's got her arms wrapped tight around herself, pulling the fabric of her jacket. There's a singed tear she might not have even noticed herself. "I'm positive I saw a gas station a mile or two back. I can head there—"

"At midnight? We'll be lucky if they're open at dawn."

Laura nods. "Then we'll bunk here for the night. If that's all right?"

It's more than all right for Amelia. But instead she says, "I guess there isn't much of a choice."

"You seem to know quite a bit about cars." Laura's sitting in the front seat—back ramrod straight, gun nestled in her lap.

Amelia's lounging in the back. She's kicked her shoes off and is resting her feet by the headrest. The rain beats against the windshield and finds its way in through the bullet holes. "Dad was a mechanic."

That earns something like a rueful smile. "Learned at his knee then?"

"Something like that." She taps Laura with a toe. "What about you? How's a nice girl from Connecticut go and become a spy?"

"Agent," she says absentmindedly.

"They recruiting out of boarding schools, or you get lost on the way to cotillion?"

"I have a talent for languages, can aim a gun, and wasn't afraid to be thrown out of a plane into the middle of France." She ducks her head. "Being a woman helped, too. Less suspicious to the Nazis."

"So you were… in the Resistance?"

She's heard about it. To a lot of people, it's a bit romantic. Brave Frenchies fighting for freedom.

"For a time."

"But you said you worked in that factory during the war."

Laura says nothing.

"Were you not supposed to tell me?"

"The majority of my war record's no secret. And I do work there now. Not much place for women in intelligence now—allegedly."

"So why'd you lie?" Amelia asks softly.

And this moment—it's one question Laura can ignore. She can play it dumb, act like she couldn't hear. Amelia's given her that out. She spoke soft enough, and the storm is loud enough.

But instead Laura's sad. Maybe melancholic is more appropriate. When she does speak it comes out honest-like. "I don't know."

Only that isn't good enough for Amelia. She moves forward throwing her arms over the front seat and hugging it. "Doesn't that bother you, Laura? Lying all the time?"

Something flickers in her eyes and Laura looks down at her pistol. "It's the job."

There. Another crack. The tiniest.

"Maybe during the war, but gab about the Russians all you like—war's over now."

"We think that? Don't we. We win a battle. Stop a Nazi. Kill a fascist. War's over. Fantastic job, kids. Pack up and move on. It's not over."

"Yeah, it is Laura. Hitler put a bullet in his head, and you all got to come home."

Laura's thumb is on the trigger of the gun she's holding. Short trimmed nail glossing over shiny metal. Brushing against the safety. Running over the roughness of the grip.

Her lips move, forming something like a sigh.

Amelia scoots closer.

She starts to reach out to Laura. Maybe put a warm hand on her damn shoulder and stave off the melancholy bringing her down. Only Laura looks up suddenly. Eyes dark. Hot. Heavy.

Laura stares, and Amelia swallows.

Then falls back against her seat. "You all got to come home. But not him. Right?"

Laura looks away again, and Amelia's half proud she hit it on the head.

"You told me about him," she adds. That blade again, rutting against all that armor, hunting for a crack.

"I told you a man died," Laura snaps.

There. A chink in it.

"Fella you love dies. You don't got a monopoly on that particular story."

It's the smile. The last vestige of Laura's armor that turns her whole profile vicious.

"He was an artist. And he was kind. And they pulled the nails from his fingers and the teeth from his mouth, and then they went to hang him in the square while we all watched."

The gun's loud as Laura drops it in the seat next to her.

"I shot him."

She's falling now. So fast. All that armor tempered in coffee and Seven Sister schooling and war is splintering.

"He smiled when he died."

"And you thought what the hell—better go with him."

She whips around so fast the car rocks. Glares at Amelia like she's been carving swastikas in the seat.

But that just...It fires Amelia up, and she sits forward again. Leans in close enough she can watch the damp cling to Laura's neck. "Fella you loved died, and it's gotta hurt like hell that you're the one that put him in his grave. But then you went and won a war. You got all that peace he lost his life over, and all you've done is squandered it. Beatin' men in pool halls. Stringing along your Frenchman. Lying to me."

That last one flies out of her with an embarrassing amount of hurt.

"It was to protect you. All of you. After him—"

"You gave up." The wind whistles as it pushes against those holes in the window. "The way I see it," she's real quiet, "There's no point in protecting the world if you don't get to live in it. And honey, you haven't lived in it since the gallows."

Laura's eyes are as dark as those fields out there. Near to black. As quick as Amelia thought she'd torn that armor down, Laura's got it back up again. She's staring at Amelia so hard she might just go up in flames.

"What do you suggest I do," Laura asks. Iron. But fresh out of the forge. Scorching.

Amelia's blood is running hot, but it feels a little pleasant, and something nervous and nice is boiling inside of her all at once. She swallows, and Laura's eyes flicker to her throat.

"Live," she finally whispers.

Laura keeps staring. And Amelia feels sick and stupid and raw.

Suddenly Laura throws the door open and bursts out of the car. She slams it behind her, leaving Amelia in deafening silence.

She scoots back. Pushing herself across the seat 'til the door handle presses into her back.

Laura stalks through the rain to the rear door.

The door opens and the rain slips in.

All she can see is Laura from the neck down. The wet's cut straight through her silk blouse and beads on the wool of her skirt.

Then she's in the car. Poised like a cat. Hand on the headrest, bracing herself up. Soaked through.

Laura's not so scary when she's bedraggled. Her makeup is near gone, and her hair's ruined. Like a puppy pulled out of the river.

She's not so scary.

But oh, that look.

Amelia swallows.

Quite of their own volition, her legs—up on the bench in front of her—part. She maybe sighs. She can't be sure of anything anymore. On account of this hungry and devastating creature, looming there, half out in the rain.

She swallows. "You're letting the wet in." Her throat sounds dry and scratchy.

Laura's almost violent the way she surges forward. She's this carnal creature that would turn Amelia's legs to jelly if she were standing. She presses into the door and struggles so hard not to kiss those lips.

Laura hovers over her and smells like rain and day old perfume. All that armor washed away completely.

Maybe it'll build back up tomorrow. Amelia can't be sure. But tonight, in a Cadillac in the middle of Jersey, it's gone.

And she's not one to brag about conquests, because it creeps her out when her cousins or brother do it, but she's kissed a lot of girls.

None of 'em ever kissed the way Laura does.

The world's not supposed to end in a kiss. All that important reality isn't supposed to feel like it's crashing down around 'em.

But kissing Laura sends the rest of the world on its way.

Laura braces herself on one hand, and the other finds its way to Amelia's bare leg. Fingertips honest to God dance up her calf and play at her knee, and she has to stop kissing just to tug on Laura's ear with her teeth and say, "The door's still open."

One of her legs moves, followed by a thump, and the outside is shut away.

Laura stops kissing her and presses her nose, all cold, to Amelia's throat. Her fingers are still on her leg. Dragging real slow.

Up.

And down.

Climbing higher.

But slow.

Laura's a nibbler, but she's real confident about it. It's all part of that sweet build. Between her mouth and her hands, she's stoking Amelia like a goddamned fire.

"Laura." She gasps, pulling on Laura's shoulders. Trying not to flail from what's building, she wraps her fingers around her wrist. "If you don't touch me soon, I'm gonna—"

Two fingers. Maybe three. Who's counting. All she knows is, Laura thrusts up into her and catches her gasp in her mouth and oh Lord.

Oh Lord, the woman's good at this.

Amelia has been crushing on Laura so long. She's never actually thought about the sex—just assumed she'd be like every other good girl who's come along.

But Laura gets it. God does she—Amelia needs more than that hand pumping in and out of her and that goddamned thumb of Laura's fluttering across her.

She needs skin. Hot, damp skin. She claws at Laura's shirt, pulls at the buttons, and forces Laura back until Amelia can straddle her thighs and have it all.

Just like the girls in the magazines.

Amelia's never understood the appeal of boys. She gets how it's easier—that's why she tried her hand at one—but really she doesn't get it. They've got no stamina compared to girls. And the hair. All that hair on their chests and arms and backs.

Laura, unlike boys, is smooth. Her breasts aren't hidden behind a thatch of blonde to match the one between her legs. And while the reflection is crummy, she still gets an idea of the muscles in Laura's back when she's over her and kissing her between nips and teasing smiles.

And she can go for hours.

They can go for hours.

Okay, maybe Laura's a little worn out. She's lying on her back, playing with Amelia's hair, and smiling like she's got a happy secret.

Amelia, being younger and having not recently engaged in any fights with other spies, has a bit more energy. She's down on the floorboard with one of Laura's legs thrown over her shoulder, enjoying a very lazy bit of cunnilingus.

Laura's bare chest is glowing with sweat. It could be love, the way Laura's looking at her.

Could be lust, too.

She slips a finger into Laura, and her eyes close. She sighs, taking the air deep into her chest. Amelia pauses just long enough to kiss her thigh.

"Feel it," she asks.

Laura just tugs her lower lip into her mouth and nods.

"Let it come."

She doesn't even need to add another finger. She could probably just blow and Laura'd come. She's real careful, letting the orgasm creep up on Laura. It's slow and easy. For seconds that seem to span hours, there's just dark hooded eyes watching her, the smell of Laura, and the pulse of her against Amelia's mouth.

It's gotta be the closest a hellbound gal like her is ever gonna get to heaven.

Laura uses her handhold in Amelia's hair to pull her up. The kisses they share, all naked and happy, are lazy and easy too. Like they've been kissing each other all their lives.

They don't talk.

They cuddle.

Amelia pillows her head on Laura's, and it isn't hard to nuzzle into her cleavage and say, "This is nice."

The hand combing through her hair pauses. Then goes back to what it was doing, nails scraping all pleasant against her scalp. "It is."

"It's not gonna last. Is it?"

"No." Laura's so quiet, Amelia could have imagined her talking if she hadn't felt it through her chest.

"The way I see it," she squeezes Laura tight, "we can wallow in what's coming. Or we can enjoy today."

Laura laughs. "You sound like the war's back on."

"A couple of hours ago, you said it never ended." She shrugs against her. "So let's think about how great the sex is gonna be when it's over."

Laura tilts Amelia's head so she has to look at her. It's gonna be a long hard road to forget those eyes. "If it doesn't?"

"We live right next door to each other, Laura. You come by for sugar, and I'll declare it Armistice Day."

She laughs, and Amelia laughs, and until the sun comes up, the war is over.

CHAPTER 8

A LIMP ALONG TO THE GAS station with a near empty tank is bad enough, but every time Amelia and Laura look at each other, they grin and giggle.

They had sex most of the night and then cuddled naked in the back of the car until well past dawn. And it shows. Between the two of them, they found exactly three hair pins, so their hair is down, two buttons are missing from Laura's shirt, and Amelia's dress is so wrinkled they might never let her back into the hotel.

And every ounce of makeup they were wearing has been kissed away.

Laura's never been more beautiful, and she says the same about Amelia when she looks at her like she hung the moon.

She kinda wants to hold Laura's hand, but she knows that's the sort of thing the girls who call home crying every night do. Instead, she sits on her fingers and bites her lip whenever the car jostles, and remembers how good her night was.

They finally roll into the gas station—"Exactly two miles," Laura crows—on fumes and prayers. While the attendant fills them up, Laura goes inside to make a phone call.

Amelia takes the moment—her first bit of alone time since an assassin tried to grab her—to just be. She lets all the bad stuff and all the good stuff settle over her like a blanket.

A lot's happened in the span of a night, and she has to figure out a way to make sense—shit!

She scoots down low and peeks carefully out the window.

A black Pontiac's rolled into the station full of no-good guys in suits. It drives slow like a glacier, inching past their stolen Cadillac while the fellas inside study it real close.

As she's been doing a lot lately, she prays. This time that the Pontiac will keep on driving.

It doesn't. Its brakes creak as it comes to a stop.

All four men exit and two head inside. The other two squint as they try and see who's in the car. One stops to talk to the attendant. The other puts his hand on his hip. Next to the holstered gun.

There are, of course, options. But the option that presents itself to Amelia, the one that makes the most sense, is the one where she slides into the driver's seat, wrenches the car into drive, and smacks the front end of the Cadillac into a man in a suit.

The other fella, the one who's talking to the attendant and making the poor kid sweat, shouts.

Which is a perfectly reasonable response to seeing your friend smacked with the front end of a Cadillac.

She pops the car into reverse. Goes back a good twenty feet. She gives the gas station a quick glance. Laura's holding her own, beating one guy with a tire iron while the other stumbles around, clutching his noggin.

She guns it into drive, screeches to a halt at the door, and leans on the horn. Laura slams the tire iron down once more for good measure and struts toward the door like the two fellas outside aren't drawing their guns and trying to load the Cadillac full of bullet holes.

Laura slides in and says, "Move over." Her tone is a little too imperious for Amelia's ego.

Amelia ignores her, puts the Cadillac back into reverse and swings the whole car around the gas pumps so the back end runs into the guys with guns. They both go down.

"Yeah right. I saw the way you drive," she says.

One of the fellas from inside the gas station stumbles out the door with his gun drawn. Amelia doesn't flinch at the bullets.

That earns a suspicious look from Laura, particularly when she smoothly brings them back onto the road and sails through the light traffic like a fish in water.

"Amelia, dear, do you have something to tell me?"

"What? So you're the only one who's got secrets?"

"Mine involve national security." They swerve around a milk truck. "Where exactly did you learn to drive like this?"

She checks the side mirror. The Pontiac is coming in fast. "We should have stopped to shoot out their tires."

Laura turns to see what the fuss is about and mutters, "Aw hell."

She pulls her gun from the glove box and checks the clip. "I've got four bullets and excellent aim. Do you think you can keep us steady?"

Okay, now Amelia is just insulted. "I'll do you one better."

She jams her foot on the brake. Smoke blooms as the brakes lock up and the whole car goes into a skid. Amelia controls the skid, and spins the car around so it's perpendicular to oncoming traffic. In particular, to the Pontiac.

This gives Laura her shot.

It also, maybe, puts Laura in the threat of being crushed under a ton or two of American steel, but the shot set up is so golden that she really shouldn't complain.

It's just a *pop pop*. Then Laura's looking at her like she's gonna say "are you quite finished." The Pontiac veers off the road into a ditch, its two front tires burst like grapes.

Amelia grins.

"I'm presuming it's something to do with your uncle's line of work. Because you were only a cab driver for three months." Laura directs her north, and then toward Long Island. "We can skip Manhattan entirely," she says, as she taps her chin. "Are you still involved in organized crime or was it a youthful indiscretion?"

"It's old news, Laura." Amelia keeps her eyes on the road.

"I don't know about that. Besides, turnabout's fair play, Amelia." The way Laura's got her tongue caught between her teeth as she grins makes Amelia want to pull the car over and play at Armistice Day some more.

She huffs. "Remember my brother living out in Nebraska?"

"The one who missed out on the draft because…" Laura waves down at her leg.

"Right. He didn't lose his leg fixing cars in the shop." She sucks in a breath through her teeth. "He got shot in the leg while knocking over a bank."

Laura's a smart lady and quickly puts two and two and three together. "And you were the getaway driver."

She nods.

"Just the once or…" She absorbs the glance Amelia shoots her. "Ah. So you two used to rob banks."

"I was a kid." It's not a great excuse. She was sixteen, it was the Depression, and she had a lot to prove to people who didn't really care. And it was *fun*.

"Sure."

"Laura. Come on—"

She waves her off. "I'm teasing, Amelia. While I'll admit to being surprised, I can hardly judge you for knocking over a few banks—"

"Eight."

Laura looks like someone hit her in the face with a frying pan. "Eight banks." She shakes her head. "How did you get away with robbing eight banks?"

"Great driver?"

"For fuck's sake."

"And we didn't all get away." The smell of rot from her brother's leg—festering from a bullet—still sits in her nose. Is gonna sit there forever, maybe.

Same with his screams as a quack sawed through bone and gristle to save his life.

"I thought I was the rebel in this car for parachuting into France."

"Don't worry. You still throw a punch better than I do."

"What led to the end of your little 'spree'?"

"Your bank robbing buddy loses his leg. It kinda takes the wind out of your sails. Dad dying didn't help. My mom… It was a rough time for her."

"And you?" Laura surveys her like she's looking for scars she missed when they were stark naked. "Couldn't have been easy."

"I'm alive, aren't I? Whole?" There's gotta be something edgy and harsh in how she says it. Something sharp.

Because Laura's trying to be consolatory. "I think we never can escape our past unscathed." She's careful. Like she's in a mine field without one of those wands the boys use. "And while I have, on more than one occasion, very much wanted to, I don't think we should either."

Coming out of that mouth, laced with that fancy Connecticut accent of hers, Laura's words could sound really condescending. But she's watching Amelia with a kind of empathy that screams "been there and done that, honey."

So Amelia nods. "What doesn't kill us, makes us stronger, huh?"

A watery laugh. "Maybe not stronger. Wiser."

"Yeah?"

Laura's smiling like she's got a secret, like her own past has informed every little action she's taken right up to and including banging Amelia's brains out in the back of a stolen Cadillac. "Yeah."

Laura's directions aren't half bad, and they end up at a fancy estate that's all marble and glass and crazy shaped topiaries. The incredulous look Amelia shoots Laura makes her blush.

"I'll admit Michel's father's choice of decor is... ostentatious."

"Please tell me he's got a statue of himself in the pond."

"How do you know about the pond?"

Place this big in Long Island, filled with that many topiaries, always has a pond. And pools. And a garage full of cars that has the grease-monkey side of her positively moist.

That's where they leave their bullet-riddled Cadillac. "I'll have Michel dispose of it later today. And see to the reimbursement of its owner."

"Thoughtful."

"Michel's father was a bit of a profiteer during the war. And he is forever grateful I saved his son from a Nazi 'hotel.' It won't be a problem."

Amelia's heard only mutterings about the hotels. Places where good people were tortured until they coughed up every secret in their head.

Not the kind of place she'd want to spend the night.

The door between the garage and the house opens wide, and Amelia is introduced to a whole new side of Tall, Dark, and French. His shirt sleeves are rolled to the elbow, and he's wearing an apron half covered in flour. Amelia does a double take.

"Michel," Laura says officiously.

Michel looks from Laura to Amelia to their hands and back to Laura again. "I was beginning to worry."

Laura and Michel have a rhythm to their banter, and Amelia doesn't even try to intervene. She stuffs her face with fresh baked pastries, knocks back coffee strong enough to make her eyes cross, and listens with rapt attention as they discuss the roll of film burning a hole in Amelia's pocket, along with mobsters and cadres of spies operating on US soil.

"What the heck is a cadre anyways?"

"A group," Laura says rather distractedly.

"*Juste*," Michel says, his mouth doing really nice things to that French word. "A group that has set their sights on you."

Laura looks pissed, but Amelia just feels a little ashamed. She robbed eight banks in 1936 and was never caught. Being outed by some lousy spies she's never met is just ridiculous.

Stupid dead Jimmy Andronico.

"At least I've a clue who they are," Laura says.

"Russians," Amelia says around some pastry.

"Yes. Russians, trying to make a deal with Italian communists through your uncle." Laura places a lot of emphasis on that connection.

Amelia has heard tell of her uncle's connections back in Italy. The Mafia connection no one ever talks about. The ones who were looking to end the fascist reign so the communists could take their place. "My uncle may not like me, but he's not gonna kill me."

"He might not have a choice. Right now, he's failed his employers and will need to prove himself. As long as you've got the film, you're a very handsome target."

"Then we toss the film in that fire—"

A very unmanly gasp escapes Michel's lips.

Laura purses her own lips. "That doesn't solve the problem either."

"So what—give it over to the communists?"

Michel starts muttering in low French, and Laura shoots him a scathing look. Scorching enough that the big baguette blushes and leaves the room, tray and cups in tow.

"More like use it to set a trap for them," Laura says. Sort of like most folks say "I went to the market for some eggs."

"You want to trap the spies who want to kill me?"

"Yes. At the very least, if I make it clear *I* have the film and you don't, their interest in you will disappear."

"Because it'll be on you."

She smirks. It's this goddamn gorgeous cocky little thing. "I'm used to being a target. Setting a trap won't be difficult."

"With who? Me and the chef?"

"I'm not the only one left out in the cold. There are quite a few of us and an op like this…It could be just the thing we need to prove that dissolving the OSS was a mistake."

The OSS—Amelia feels like someone's sitting on her chest. Or maybe she's got her whole hand in there. Squeezing. "You want the film so you can get a job?" She's really impressed with how she doesn't raise her voice.

Laura shakes her head like she means what she says next. "No, that's merely an additional reason. I want the film so I can keep you safe."

"How're you supposed to keep me safe from a faceless cadre of spies?"

"For one thing, they're not faceless. One of them infiltrated the hotel."

She raises her eyebrow, but more at Laura using a word like *infiltrated*. "One of 'em was in the Sebastian?"

"Judy from 2E is in New York for more than stardom and excellent bagels."

"Judy…*Hayseed* is a spy? Woman still hasn't seen the Atlantic."

"Woman is very good at lying. And an excellent spy, judging by her assassination attempt. I didn't even suspect her until last night."

"What changed your mind? She start humming the Soviet Anthem?"

"Saw her face when she tried to shoot mine off."

Fair enough.

Laura continues, "Now that I know who she is and I have what she wants, it's just a matter of setting her up. I have all the cards."

"*We* have all the cards."

"Of course. But," Laura huffs, "Amelia, we can't—you can't—this has to be delicate."

"I can be delicate." She sounds defensive. Which is stupid, because she can be delicate. She's done it at least twice in her life.

Laura sighs. "I'm not saying you can't."

"You just did!"

Laura breathes in deep through her nose. She looks worn out. She often does. Amelia gets that the whole world sits on her shoulders and pulls her down with the weight of it. Their little chats at the diner. What happened in the car. Amelia herself. They're nothing more than respites from a world Laura feels too responsible for. "The war isn't over." She would remind Amelia if she said anything.

So Amelia doesn't.

They sit there in one of the most uncomfortable silences Amelia's ever suffered through. Laura looks at her with all the pain and weariness she's been carrying around since the war, and Amelia tries to ignore all the unsaid stuff she never wants to hear.

Then. Then Laura goes and breaks the silence, and it's with a mere whisper of Amelia's name.

She hangs her head, and all of Laura's weariness crawls up onto Amelia's shoulders, too. "You really don't want me to come, do you?"

"This operation—it's so dangerous, Amelia. More than anything you could have—"

"So I play damsel in the tower, while you go off and fight the dragon."

"I have experience."

"I do too!"

"Robbing banks! Dealing with mobsters. I would think, after what you've seen, you'd realize that this is two different worlds we're talking about." She's been sitting on the couch opposite Amelia, and she leans back on it, arms crossed in a very final kind of way, chin jerked up like a snob. "And you are simply not equipped for mine."

As much as Amelia wants to pop Laura in the mouth or maybe flounce out of the room, steal one of those cars, and do things all on her own. She doesn't. She stands up and comes over and kneels on the floor by Laura. She curls her hand around Laura's knee, looks up at her, and speaks real soft. Intimate. "So equip me."

Laura closes her eyes.

Breathes in long and slow.

"You've got to know I want to."

"Nothing's stopping you. Nothing but your own stubbornness."

Laura doesn't agree. She frowns in a way that's enough to break a heart. "People who come into my world—who even flirt with it—have a bad habit of not making it out." Her hand cups Amelia's chin, and she gently pulls her up so Amelia's leaning over her. Holding herself up with a hand on the arm of the couch. Laura clearly wants to put their foreheads together. Maybe kiss her softly.

Amelia really wants her to, too. But she doesn't cross those last couple of inches. This gap between them is the only bargaining chip she's got. "I'm not like the rest of 'em, Laura."

It's unspoken, but both of them know what that gap means. What crossing it'll do. But Laura crosses it anyways. Leans up and kisses her. Words like gossamer come to mind when she presses her lips so gently to Amelia's.

"That's what he said too—before he died."

Getting compared to a guy dead in France.

Amelia gets...She gets sleepy. Truth be told, she's been sleepy. But now it's pulling at her insistently. Tugging on her brain and body.

Her arms grow heavy. Her eyelids don't want to stay open. She droops.

Laura stands to catch her. Soothes her with gentle hands and words.

"What—"

"Your coffee. I knew you'd insist on coming."

She curses as Laura carefully spins her and lays her gently on the couch.

"I can't disagree," Laura says. "But I can't lose you either."

It's maybe the worst thing that's ever happened in Amelia's whole life, because Laura leans down and kisses her on the cheek. "I think I might love you too much for that."

Of all the lousy, no good, romantic, stupid, wonderful things to s...

CHAPTER 9

THE MAJORITY OF PEOPLE DON'T find drugging a person particularly romantic.

It is, in fact, presumptuous. And a little cruel.

Possibly also illegal.

Almost certainly illegal.

Nevertheless, Laura finds herself with few options. She could take her lover with her to a meeting that would surely end in death, she could lock her up—but knowing Amelia that would work for an hour at most—or she could drug her into unconsciousness and work hard not to marvel at how peaceful Amelia looks while asleep.

Sleeping people normally remind Laura of the dead. The stillness. The closed eyes. The slack mouths. She sees someone slumbering and can only see the bodies stacked like logs after a round of executions.

But Amelia is still very much alive, and Laura could sit on the couch watching the soft flutter of her eyelids and the careful tick of her lips for the rest of her waking days. Except lurking around Michel's father's estate, watching Amelia sleep, won't solve a damn thing.

Laura stokes the fire crackling in the fireplace, carefully leaves the room, and pulls the door shut behind her.

Michel waits for her in the kitchen. His shirtsleeves are rolled up past his elbows, and he's cleaning the glut of pans he's made a mess of while baking. "How's your friend," he asks. There's a hardness that rests on the word "friend." A mild accusation he really has no right to make.

"Asleep." She's terser than she should be, and she knows it. Dear Michel has gone out of his way to help her with her work. Driving for her, covering for her, even housing her. It shouldn't matter that so much of his helpfulness is related to his affection for her.

"It's love," he claimed once. She'd kissed the corner of his mouth and told him it would only ever be a one-sided affair. That was years ago, when she was mad for his brother. Before both she and Michel had lost him to Nazi gallows.

He would have hated what she'd just done. Would have looked upon her with revulsion—just like Amelia will if they ever see one another again.

But Michel doesn't, does he? He's never repulsed by the actions Laura takes. Even thanked her when she shot his brother. "You saved him from suffering," he said at the time. "No one else could have managed."

Michel understands her, understands the callous and cruel creature she can be.

She packs her pistol and the roll of film into her purse and shoulders it. "Can you—" She tries very hard not to sigh. "Can you watch her? While I'm gone?"

Michel nods. "Anything for you," the gesture says.

He calls after her, still not turning from the sink. "And if she wakes up? What would you have me say?"

There's the noise of the washing. Water sloshing and suds striking the sides of the ceramic sink.

"Tell her I'm sorry, won't you?"

He stops washing but doesn't look at her.

"And that…All I wanted to do was keep her safe."

A dead man swinging on the gallows is there between her and him again. A ghostly visage lurking only in their minds' eyes.

Michel doesn't have to ask if Laura's feelings for Amelia are anything like her feelings for his dead brother. But what Laura truly loves about Michel is that he won't ask either.

Amelia's uncle lives in South Brooklyn, which isn't, technically, the southern most part of Brooklyn. It's just what everyone calls the part south of downtown when they don't want to use the name Red Hook. That moniker sounds more dangerous. Violent. Much like the man Laura's come from Long Island to see.

Vince Pedrotti has his fingers in an awful lot of pies, but his biggest success is in import and export. With his connections at the docks, he can get anyone he wants out of the country. And he can get anything he wants in.

And that's exactly how a film canister full of Nazi secrets made its way into New York.

She wonders if he knows who he's working for. If he understands how he's trading Nazi secrets to communists.

It's one of the two things she's come all the way out to South Brooklyn to ask.

The old man takes his time coming to the door, his shadow on the glass moving at an unhurried shuffle.

Bad hip. Must get stiff when he sits for too long.

So why has he been sitting all day? Waiting by the phone perhaps?

She gently rests a hand on the flap of her purse and stands as tall as she can.

Locks click, one after the other, and then the door opens. A record's playing in another room. Strains of some melancholic opera filter through, and if Laura cared about such things, she might even be able to name it.

Pedrotti sighs when he finds her waiting for him. Steps aside and lets her in. "If you've come to kill me, sweetheart, then you better have more than a peashooter in that purse."

She feigns surprise. "Why on earth do you think I want to kill you?"

"Was you who killed my men the other day, wasn't it?"

She laughs and walks into the house as though she owns it. Takes a seat in a green velvet chair in the parlor. "I suppose introductions aren't necessary."

"Didn't say that. I know what you've done. Still don't know who exactly you are."

"Then I have the advantage, Mr. Pedrotti, because I'm one of the very few people in this opera to know all the players."

He scowls, and it should be menacing, but Laura's faced down men who've ordered the deaths of millions. Pedrotti's list of condemned is much shorter. Maybe just a hundred. He can't compare.

"Like my niece."

"Amelia's been dragged into this, and I think we can both agree that's a mistake."

He sucks on the inside of his cheek, dark eyes appraising her like a shipping manifest. "You know what she used to do? Before all this acting business?"

"She's mentioned it."

He sinks down into a hard looking wooden chair opposite her. The finish has worn off the arm rests and the chair creaks with Pedrotti's weight. The way he settles, the way the palms of his hands work at those worn spots, tells her it's his chair. The throne from which he dispenses all his judgments.

"Smartest one of her whole little gang. A real talent. Could have been famous the way she drives. But her brother lost his leg, and the girl lost her taste for it."

"Tragedy tends to do that." Or it's supposed to. A lover swinging from the gallows, bullet hole smoking in his chest… that's supposed to scare a woman away.

"And I don't know you, but I know enough to know you like what you do. The way you did those boys down at that bar, you'd have to love it."

"No allowances for mere talent?"

His laugh is more the weary sigh of the very old. "Talent don't mean everything. That's why my niece isn't famous yet."

"Well…" She methodically smooths her skirt out over her thighs. It's wrinkled from being worn too long, and there are stains from last night's rain around the hem. "You're right. Despite talent, this isn't Amelia's world. It's mine and yours." She plucks at the weave and glances up through her eyelashes. "And the world of the communists you've been doing business with."

It's quite coy.

Pedrotti hisses, drawing a breath in through yellowed teeth. "Didn't know that at the time. Just supposed to be helping out a friend of a friend. They weren't fascists, so I figured it was fine."

"Fascists are far too 1945. We're in 1946, and communists are persona non grata. Smuggling secrets for the communists is even worse. Traitorous, some might say."

He clenches his jaw, and the action pulls the wrinkled skin taut across bulging tendons. "You keep saying that word in my company, Miss, and you're the one that's gonna end up dead."

She's certainly hit a mark. The man wouldn't be so ashamed if he'd known from the beginning whom he was working for.

"You can try to kill me, but I highly doubt you have anyone in your employ that's capable of the feat." She leans forward, her elbows digging into the meat of her legs. "However, I'm not here just to talk about your communist friends and traitorous acts—"

"I love this country."

"Enough to betray it to Russia, Mr. Pedrotti." She says his name clearly, with that inflection reserved for the hard of hearing. It's the officious tone she reserves for those who need to be patronized. "Now, I had two reasons for coming here."

"To call me a traitor."

She nods. "And for Amelia's sake. She needs protection."

"You care about her." Between people like them, killers, that's an accusation.

And one they should both be subject to. "So do you." If he didn't, Amelia's body would have wound up in the Gowanus Canal the first moment she started asking questions.

"You want my promise not to kill her," he says.

"No, I want your promise to *protect* her. Whatever happens over the course of the next few days, I need to know you'll keep her alive."

"Long as she's got that film, there's not a damn thing I can do for her."

"Well," Laura reaches into her purse and produces the film, "it's a good thing she doesn't have it then." She sets it on the coffee table between them. Pedrotti stares at it as a hungry man might stare at a sandwich.

"Calling me a traitor, and you're sitting here ready to deal for a girl's life?"

She slips the film back into her purse. "I've already seen how deals you arrange turn out. I'll be dealing with the communists personally."

"I can't arrange that."

"I didn't ask you to. I *asked* you to keep Amelia safe. You've seen the film, and you know she doesn't have it. There's no reason she needs to die now."

"I—"

"Can promise it. I know you can, because as powerful as these people are, they still don't know this city like you do. If they did, Amelia would already be dead. And you would too."

The opera in the other room ends, and is replaced by the hiss of white noise from the speakers. "You're honestly just here to secure her protection, aren't you? The film and spies, it's all secondary."

"Yes." Why is that even a question?

He chuckles. Actually *chuckles*. The life of his niece is on the line and the man is laughing. "Jesus. I knew she was crazy, looking after you like the two of you are going steady, but you're just as perverted as her, aren't you?"

Other than some behind-closed-doors, very quiet interactions with other girls in school, Laura had never really considered... being with another woman. Of course she'd *done* it, but she'd never thought much of it. She'd certainly never explored the culture—not like Amelia.

So, this is the first time anyone has ever looked her in the eye and called her a pervert.

It is... unsettling. Not quite like being called a "dame" in a group of men. That's something she's been dealing with her whole life. This is a surprise.

It never really occurred to her that she's "perverted" simply because she cares for Amelia. Yes, it is very different, mechanically speaking, from a relationship with a man. But it is theirs, and it is private. To be honest, Laura feels like laughing.

A pervert?

Then she remembers Amelia. Remembers the shame carried in every one of her lustful glances.

It's all absurd to Laura, but to Amelia, the word—and all the feelings behind it—is a violent insult.

One she's suffered from her own family's lips on more than one occasion.

Laura has to resist the very strong impulse to pull her gun out and shoot Pedrotti in the leg. She also has to resist the urge to lunge across the coffee table and wrap her fingers around his throat.

She pops one of her knuckles with her thumb.

Glares.

That's enough to turn Pedrotti wan.

He clears his throat. Looks away. *Relents.* "I'll keep her safe."

"Good," she says very evenly.

When she leaves, after milking Pedrotti for all the intel she can, he walks her to the door.

He's put on another opera, and it soars.

"You know, you never told me your name," he says. It's a conversational tone. Meant to endear him to her. It's also very clumsy.

At least for a spy. "No, I certainly didn't."

"You going to? Ought to know the name of a woman I'm doing a favor for."

"The favor is for your niece, Mr. Pedrotti, and if she doesn't survive the night, I guarantee you won't survive the week."

"Bit of a mouthful of a name."

Laura walks away. She'd really rather not have Vince Pedrotti see her smile. It's not even the bad joke, or Pedrotti himself, that stirs up amusement. It's the way he said it.

Just like Amelia would.

CHAPTER 10

Laura's plan is incredibly daring and noble. It is also incredibly stupid. If the man who put her onto this mission in the first place knew what she is risking—if her own former commanders knew—she'd be strung up. Or drummed out. Or driven farther into the ground than she already is.

Setting traps is dangerous. Settings traps with almost no support and absolutely no contingency plan is downright suicidal.

She takes the train from Brooklyn back into the city. Returns to the Sebastian with just the gun and the film in her purse.

Two men sit in a Pontiac opposite the hotel, and their glares are all too knowing. If they could snatch her off the street right then, they would. Snatch her up and take her away to some warehouse where they'd torture her until she gave up every secret she's ever known.

She ignores them, just as she ignored her own people. The ones she called from Pedrotti's place. They're in another car farther up the street, sitting low in their seats and using their mirrors to watch the Pontiac boys. They're good at what they do, and they'll keep Judy's friends out of Laura's way.

Which is all she needs. A little help to watch her back.

With her head held high, she walks into the hotel she's called home.

Moving into the Sebastian Hotel for Young Women wasn't her first choice. In France she'd had her own small apartment, and she'd hoped to have the same back in the States. Unfortunately, everyone else returning from the war had the same bright idea. The city was filled to bursting and demand for apartments was high, as was the rent.

The city was also tremendously *lonely*. She didn't have a group of ready-made friends in the form of a resistance cell. Didn't even have the camaraderie of the OSS. All she had was the louts at work who eyed her with wary lust, plus a few old intelligence friends who were usually too busy to chat.

The Sebastian was a ready-made group of friends. Girls who did each other's nails, grumbled about love and looked out for one another.

Girls who drank schnapps together.

The Sebastian gave her Amelia, who stormed into her life with a cocky grin and a sharp knock on the door. "How ya doing," she asked, held out her hand, and dared Laura not to shake it.

While the other girls quickly shied away from Laura, Amelia doubled down. She invited her to the diner for free coffee and insisted on dragging her out to the pictures. She laced their fingers together, wrapped her other hand around Laura's arm, and listened to every bit of idiocy that stuttered out of Laura's mouth.

In so many ways, Amelia saved Laura's life over the last year. She built her up when it seemed the whole rest of the world conspired to beat her down.

In those early days, falling in love with Amelia felt inevitable.

In the present, all Laura can do is curse her own tardiness. If she said something sooner—moved faster—she and Amelia might have had more than one exquisite night and an awful good-bye.

It's the only regret she can allow to haunt her.

Laying traps requires a clear mind, and Amelia's smile just muddies that.

The sun is well on its way to setting, and light the color of orange sherbet is lancing in through the windows of the hotel, chasing Laura's own dark shadow.

Mrs. Edith Myrtle is waiting for her at the foot of the stairs, her small mouth screwed up tight with disdain. "Miss Wright," she says, "I've been looking for you."

"Have you?" Reflexively Laura's coy, but she means to be casual. Myrtle can sniff out a lie better than many professional interrogators.

"We had an incident last night in Miss Maldonado's room. Imagine my shock and concern when neither she or her neighbor could be found."

"I was in Connecticut, ma'am. Visiting my father."

Her beady little eyes narrow, and she searches Laura's face for the lie. "I was told you were in the hotel. Do you know what happened?"

"Someone sneak in a man?"

"A gun."

She feigns shock with a hand to the chest. "A gun. Here? In the Sebastian?"

"Yes. And it was fired in Miss Maldonado's room. Then someone said they saw you, Miss Wright."

"They're mistaken."

Myrtle sniffs. She doesn't have any proof, just suspicions. The night before had been hectic, all gun smoke, darkness, and screams of frightened girls.

Laura tells the hausfrau she really must go and quickly climbs the steps. She doesn't look back. That would invite Mrs. Myrtle to continue the conversation, and Laura really doesn't have the time.

The open door, an unsettling sight, gives Laura a clear viewpoint into Amelia's empty room. Her belongings are scattered everywhere, and someone has drawn chalk around the bullet holes in the wall. It is, unmistakably, a crime scene.

It's also incredibly eerie. Because, despite the mess—despite the chalk—it still smacks of Amelia. Of home.

Laura ducks her head and goes to her own room. She has to root through her purse for the keys, and she's just got the right one slotted into the lock when a figure emerges in her peripheral.

"Hi," Judy says too brightly.

If she weren't a spy who'd tried to kill Laura and Amelia the night before, she might be pretty. Her auburn hair—natural going by the tint of her eyebrows—is pulled back a little too severely, but it highlights the sharp lines of her cheekbones and sharper hook of her nose. She softens her image with the perfect application of rouge. It makes her look young. Wholesome. So, it's the eyes that do her in as a spy. Judy has watery blue eyes that bring to mind the milky ones of a blind man. And they're too wide. Too *busy*.

"Haven't seen you around," Judy says. "Everything all right?" Those eyes rove over everything, slotting away facts and clues like a file clerk.

The only leg up Laura has in this particular scenario is she knows what Judy actually is, while Judy has no idea that she knows. So, she twists her key and unlocks her door and walks in shoulder first. "Just busy," she says tightly. "Had to go up to Connecticut." She's got to sound harried. Got to sound like an accomplished spy on urgent business.

"Oh. Did... did Amelia go with you?"

She plays dumb. "No. I haven't seen her since breakfast yesterday. Is everything all right? Mrs. Myrtle mentioned a gun of all things."

"Yeah! One that went off in Amelia's room! Half the girls thought it was fireworks, but me, I grew up on a farm."

"So you knew it was a gun."

"Oh yes," Judy says. Eyes wide and guileless. She's really very good at playing this character. "Anyways, I saw you come in, and I just knew I had to ask you about it. I mean you and Amelia are so... close." Little Judy, the Russian spy, is *much* better than Laura at playing the innocent busybody. She sounds like any one of the gossips Laura went to boarding school with. There's no accusation in her statement. Not even thinly veiled insinuation.

Laura doesn't even try to be as good. She's setting a trap and needs Judy to walk into it because she thinks she's smarter than Laura.

Even though she hates it, she plays dumb. Plays the spy who thinks she's clever. "Oh." She does her best owlish blink. Tilts her head. The clever spy who has no idea how close she is to the enemy. "I'm sure Amelia's just fine. Now if you'll excuse me, Connecticut was just exhausting." The spy just begging to be kidnapped. "I think I'm due for a nap."

She steps into her room and shuts the door in Judy's face.

The bait has been set in place. Now she just needs Judy to bite.

With a wig and some clothes she needs to take to the laundry, Laura fashions a terrible looking dummy and tucks it into her bed. She leaves the lamp on next to the bed and it casts deep shadows across the room.

She stations herself in the closet and waits, her gun held loosely at her side.

She can't see the clock from her position and not enough light leaks into the closet for her to check her watch, so there's just the loud tick of both timepieces to give her any semblance of time.

She waits.

Her feet start to hurt. A burn that starts around the arches and slowly, excruciatingly, moves up past the ankles and then into the calves.

And she waits.

Her gun is heavy in her hand, and she thinks if she holds it any longer, her arm will fall off.

And she waits.

The buzz of forty girls in a hotel diminishes. They retire to their beds. Doors slam shut and do not open.

And she waits.

The light on the bedside table flickers. Stays on.

Her own door opens with not even a whisper.

Judy, the Russian spy, is really quite good at what she does. Her movements are almost enviously quiet. Hard heeled boots make no noise on the carpet and that creak Laura's never complained about in the hinge—it's an excellent early alarm system—doesn't actually creak. Judy even notices the matchstick Laura left in the door to let her know if people have been in and out of her room.

Her shoulders sag noticeably when she creeps over to the bed and realizes she's fallen for a ruse.

"Honestly, I thought you'd turn the lights out first." Laura emerges from the closet, gun carefully aimed at Judy's chest.

"Myrtle would have gotten suspicious if the lights went out two nights in a row." She speaks differently now that her secret's out. Her voice is lower. Sultry almost.

"Fair enough. We can't have your cover ruined, can we?"

Judy shrugs and turns around, hands already up in surrender. "How'd you know it was me?"

"You whipped your mask off too early last night. Saw your face as I was running away."

"It was pitch black."

"Excellent night vision."

"That why you were recruited?"

"I was recruited because of my excellent language skills." Judy starts to put her arms down.

"And," Laura continues, "because of my marksmanship. Keep your hands up please."

"They're getting tired."

"I stood in that closet with my gun out for half the night. I think you can keep your arms up for a little while longer."

Judy glances over at the bed. "Can I sit?"

Laura doesn't particularly want her to sit, because she doesn't trust Judy even a little, but Judy looks so amused at the idea that Laura doesn't trust her to sit, so Laura, naturally, *has* to give her permission. Spy games are so convoluted.

She motions with her gun, and Judy sits with a sigh.

"Know why I was recruited?" Judy says conversationally.

"I get the feeling you're about to tell me."

"I was recruited because no one would miss me."

"Low bar they set in the USSR."

"There were other factors. A gift for gab and a love of a good fight." She crosses her legs. It's rather impressive what with her hands still held up in surrender. "What I don't understand, Laura, is why you're retired."

Her aim falters, and she hopes Judy doesn't notice. "Excuse me?"

"You're an excellent agent, architect of some of the most successful components of the Resistance, and I've seen the wanted posters. The Nazis *hated* you. So why do you work floor security at a bomb factory? Shouldn't you be off in Argentina or Italy hunting the war criminals with the rest of your friends?"

"They needed some of us at home—"

"And not on the payroll."

"I'm compensated just fine."

Judy laughs. It's a rich laugh. Totally at odds with her usual "aw shucks" way of conversing. "Sure. You and all the other little girl spies. If you really want to make your old bosses happy, you ought to get married, put on an apron. Maybe have some kids."

She'd like to tell Judy to shut up, but unfortunately Judy has hit on a very sore point for Laura. One that's smarted since the OSS sent her back to the United States. It's hard to tell someone to be quiet when they're speaking the truth.

"Now, the people I work for? They're—"

"About to be short one spy if you don't shut up. I'm well aware of how irritating my government can be, but I'm not about to turn traitor because yours likes girls more."

"Why not? I'm loyal to my government, and it's loyal to me. You're loyal to your government, and you can't even afford a real apartment."

"No, but I can afford friends. Two of whom are downstairs picking up your boys in the Pontiac."

Judy blanches.

Laura grins. "It wasn't just girls out on their asses when they shuttered the OSS. And what better way to get ourselves reinstated than bringing in a big fat Soviet catch."

A spy, aware that she's caught, should promptly surrender. Or snap a cyanide capsule between her teeth. There's only ever two ways out for a caught spy. Turning traitor or dying.

Fighting is inadvisable. And she certainly shouldn't fling a wig at the gunwoman and then charge her.

But that's precisely what Judy does.

The gun gets knocked aside when Judy tackles her like a linebacker. It might be for the best. The walls of the Sebastian are thin and a stray bullet could easily kill some innocent girl.

The women grapple. Judy's efficient and trained in that bizarre Russian sambo nonsense, something Laura's never been on the other side of. All Laura has is years of brawling in bars overseas and a few delicious months of training with an Olympic boxer.

The fight is... painful. A particularly well aimed elbow makes her see stars and stumble.

That's all the impetus Judy needs to snap on the hot plate and try to force Laura's face into it.

"A hot plate, Laura? What will Mrs. Myrtle say?"

Oh God. She's one of those people who quips when she fights.

Laura grabs a handful of Judy's pragmatic little bun and yanks hard enough to hear hair ripped out. Then she gets her own elbow into the game and smashes it into Judy's ribs before she throws her back with her shoulders and rounds on her.

They both pause for a breath. Judy's grinning like a crazy woman, dancing from foot to foot, and shaking her whole body like a fighter before the bell.

Laura falls into a familiar stance and brings her hands up. She's positive she has less official training than Judy. She never went into the actual ring with the Olympian— it's unladylike—but she's grappled and beat men twice her weight and knows for a fact that her right hook has widowed at least one woman.

She's also willing to bet that she can take a blow better than Judy.

God, she hopes she can take a blow better than Judy.

Her best chance at surviving is putting Judy down fast and after three failed attempts to land a punch, she knows she needs her gun to finish the job. So she dashes for it, and Judy tries to stop her by throwing a bottle at Laura's head.

A bottle of acetone she uses when doing her nails.

When Laura ducks the throw, the bottle smashes against the wall behind her, the fumes hit the scorching hot plate, and the whole damn room goes up in flames.

CHAPTER 11

HAVING NEVER BEEN DRUGGED BEFORE, Amelia's got no idea how a person is supposed to wake up. Is she just supposed to pop awake, or is it supposed to involve lots of delicate fluttering of her eyelids and a suggestive moan?

She's pretty sure, for most people, it isn't supposed to include rolling off a couch and onto her hands and knees, followed by throwing up all the pastries she imbibed earlier in the day.

The only good part of it is, once the pastries are out of her stomach and onto the expensive carpet, she feels a whole lot better.

Then she remembers how she came to be drugged and tossing all her cookies in the first place.

Stupid gorgeous rat fink of a dame—

Nope. Still more cookies to toss.

That's when Tall, Dark, and French chooses to enter the room and is clearly horrified by the sight.

"Something not agree with you," he asks. Then he looks away, because apparently a gal hunched over her own mess is too much for a dreamy looking French fella.

"Yeah," she says. "Apparently my stomach hates getting drugged. Who knew?"

Michel frowns. "She had her reasons."

Amelia wipes her hand across her mouth. "Sure she did, but just cause she had a reason, doesn't mean it's a *good* one." She thinks about standing. "How long?"

"It's after nine now."

She tries standing, but has to stop when the room starts spinning.

"Come on." Tall, Dark, and French is suddenly standing right beside her and speaking softly. "Let's get some coffee and proper food in you."

"Don't think that'll help."

"You'd be surprised."

The coffee and food doesn't help, but stealing a car while Michel's back is turned and high tailing it back into the city sure as hell does.

She isn't exactly sure where she should head first, but she figures going to the Sebastian—or at least driving by it—is as good a plan as any. So she crosses the bridge into Manhattan with her foot glued to the gas and doesn't let up until she hits a glut of traffic six blocks from the hotel.

It's the kind of traffic that usually makes her glad she walks everywhere, but it's well after ten o'clock. The only reason traffic would be this bad after ten is if there's a crazy pile up or an exploding building or—

She gets out of the car.

—Or someone's dead.

The smell of smoke, of all the pieces of someone's home on fire, hits her worse than Laura's betrayal ever could. Her brain stops working, but her feet carry her just fine.

Down one block.

Two.

Six.

Right to the edge of an inferno she used to call home.

Girls in soot spattered robes huddle around sobbing, and Mrs. Myrtle paces the edge of the ruins as if her worrying alone will put the flames out.

People from the neighborhood have come out of their homes to watch and kids up past their bedtimes scream around Amelia's ankles like it's the Fourth of the Goddamned July.

Cops are on the scene. And firemen. Working slowly to figure out the blaze and the growing crowd.

Amelia grabs one girl by the elbow and asks her if she's seen Laura.

The girl points back at the fire that's hot on Amelia's face. "She was still inside I think? Helping Judy. Poor kid was in a bad way. Absolutely hysterical."

So why didn't one of them help? Why didn't any of them?

She must mutter the question aloud, because the girls look ashamed, and they don't try to stop her when she rushes toward the fire.

Nope. It's the fire itself that stops her. A gout of flame leaps out of what used to be the front entrance. Snatches at her dress and hair and threatens to turn her into smoke and ash too.

It's too hot. Hotter than steam off a radiator or the torch her dad used in the garage.

Hot enough that she knows she can't go in.

Because that kind of blaze—that heat. A girl won't survive. Not an aspiring actress or a Russian spy or a stupid gorgeous rat fink of a dame. That kind of heat kills whatever it touches.

Including, maybe, Amelia's last gasp at happiness.

CHAPTER 12

THINGS MOVE FAST WHEN THE fire breaks out. As fast as the fire itself—which rips across the wall as if it's coated in gasoline.

The fighting is frantic. Painful. Smoke scorches her lungs and flames dry the sweat off her brow as soon as it appears. Judy darts in again—confident in her grappling technique. The two roll through burning embers and fall out into the hallway where confused girls don't yet realize they should run.

She screams for them to go, and Judy laughs as she wraps her arm around Laura's neck and squeezes.

And squeezes.

"Go," she shouts, mocking Laura. "Run!"

Feet pound and girls flee and Laura's vision blurs.

Judy's wet lips press to Laura's ear. "You've really got to stop caring about people who can't return the favor."

She tries to hit Judy with a sharp elbow, but all that earns is a grunt.

"What do you think? After I kill you, should I tie up loose ends? Kill the mobster and his little wannabe actress niece?"

She brings her heel down on Judy's toe, but the damned woman is wearing top-notch boots that absorb the blow with ease.

"I mean, she's got to go, right? *Way* too nosy for her own good."

She gets a leg between two of Judy's and tips them both right into the fire.

The scream that rings in her ears is absolute music.

She rolls away on blistered hands and goes for the stairs. But the smoke is so thick, she can't see anything but the orange glow of the flames.

There's the laundry chute behind her. A cool smoke-free point in the inferno, but unless there's actual laundry at the end of the two story drop, it's suicide.

God her hands hurt.

They're already getting stiff.

"Bitch." Judy rolls out of the fire, panting and smelling like seared pork. "Just. You... you bitch!"

There's a quip she's tempted to make about not playing with fire.

A piece of the ceiling falls between them. A blazing line of demarcation neither can cross. Judy's polyester shirt has melted into her skin, and there's an awful burn that's crawled up her neck.

She grins. "Could use some butter for that burn." Much better quip.

Judy's fury cracks and reveals something awful and manic just beneath. She looks as though she might leap through the flames to wrap her hands around Laura's throat.

Laura reaches for the laundry chute, because if she's got to go, she'd rather it be via her own route. Judy tilts her head in warning.

Laura shrugs.

She throws herself in, and Judy's wrathful screech chases after her. Pierces her ears. The fall down the chute is just as bad. Every blow against the side forming a dull blossom of pain.

She falls forever.

And then. There's the smoke. The taste of it in her mouth. The scent of it in her nose. It forms a film on her eyes.

"Breathe."

A soft voice in her ear. Fighting through the throbbing ache in her head.

Familiar. Amelia?

"Come on sweetheart. Just take a breath."

Not Amelia. She hates the word sweetheart. Says only assholes use it.

She tries to open her eyes or take a breath, but everything is so damn hard, as if she's trapped in molasses and can't get out.

A hand presses to her chest. Cool through the thin gown she's wearing. "Just breathe."

She tries again. Focuses on her lungs and pulls air in.

It's cool and bottled tasting, canned air that moves through her and invigorates her as well as any cup of coffee.

She finally manages to open her eyes and finds herself in some sterile place. Everything is white and polished, except for the mint green tiles on the walls. Her gaze roves over them, searching for the calm voice that isn't Amelia's.

It's a nurse in a stark white uniform, with a perfectly starched hat. She smiles kindly enough. "There you are."

She reaches over Laura and adjusts the oxygen. Tells her she needs to breathe through the mask for just a little while to help her lungs.

She's a polite thing. Babbles about how Laura was found in the debris but seems to be doing well. "Frankly I'm surprised you're even awake," she says candidly.

Laura smiles.

"And your friend will be relieved. Was making an absolute ruckus in the waiting room."

She leans back against her pillow. Of course Amelia would. Probably threatening some poor doctor's kneecaps. "She's rather cross with me," she says, and her voice must be muffled by the mask because the nurse looks at her with confusion.

And then she's gone. Replaced by a doctor who talks about broken ribs and concussions and nasty burns on her hands.

Thanks to the oxygen and some cocktail of drugs dripping into her from a glass bottle, she can't feel any of that. She waves him off.

All Laura wants is to see Amelia. She knows she'll be mad. She'll come in red-faced and furious, and then she'll huff and call Laura an idiot and crawl onto the bed with her. She'll pillow Laura's head on her arm, play with her hair, and whisper about what a fool she is.

There will be kisses and teasing and that Armistice Day Amelia spoke so highly of.

But Amelia never comes. Minutes tick by, and when the door opens again, it's a tall man with a fast receding hairline, a jaw shaped like a fist, and a thin lipped smile that's more a grimace.

She recognizes him instantly. Frank Wisner.

While she was in France, he manned the intelligence war in Romania. He saved lives. And spent them like spare change.

He's back to being a lawyer now. Corporate law, making more in a week than she makes in a month.

He drops his hat onto the foot of her bed and claps. Slowly. A little patronizingly. "Good job," he says. "Couldn't have run that better myself."

Men like Frank Wisner don't run the ops.

He takes a seat in the chair by her bed and lets out a satisfied groan. The kind a gentlemen never makes in unfamiliar mixed company. Laura's not sure if she should be offended or flattered.

"Real fine job. Hear you and your boys might even get a commendation out of it."

"I—we just did what anyone would do in our circumstances."

He actually harrumphs. "You unraveled a Soviet plot on American soil with none of the resources you should have had. No, ma'am." He leans forward, legs spread wide. "What you did is extraordinary, Miss Wright. Embrace it!"

He stares at her until she smiles.

"Good girl." He slaps his leg. "I don't know about you, but it's been rough being out of the business, especially seeing who runs it now. All military men with no taste for good intelligence work."

"I'm aware."

Wisner used to be military himself. He made the move to intelligence as soon as he could. "Nice fellas, don't get me wrong, but they don't quite grasp this war we're fighting.

The last one was all explosions and right and wrong, as clear cut as a side of beef at the butcher's shop. But this new war's about putting a knife in the back instead of a bayonet in the gut. Little chillier than what they're used to."

She looks at the bandages wrapped tight around her hands. "Personally, I found it to be rather warm."

Wisner laughs as though Laura might be Laurel and Hardy all rolled into one. "Lord, I like you. Sense of humor, brain in your head, and a woman."

He says the last one as if it's a bullet point on a list of her most admirable traits. She raises an eyebrow.

"Those men in the military don't quite get this war, because they think the woman's job is done, don't they? Sent you straight home. Ignored all that work you did and all that good intelligence you gathered. Kind a man could never get."

It's a trap. It has to be. Frank Wisner is sitting at her bedside parroting everything she's ranted about herself, and that can't happen. Shouldn't happen.

So, Laura carefully says nothing. She nods, and it could be tacit agreement or polite encouragement to continue.

Either way, he keeps going. "The war that's coming—the war you just launched a salvo in—we don't need those boys."

"Mr. Wisner...Are you trying to recruit me?"

He grins, and it isn't unlike a wolf's. All teeth. "I'm just a lawyer. One who happens to recognize your cause. And your talent. Just wanted to come tell you in person how pleased I am with your service."

"I certainly appreciate it."

"But this war continues, and I've no doubt people with authority will come to call. All they have to do is look at your record to see your talent. That Frenchman you shot on the gallows? Kind of ruthlessness this war will need."

Sometimes it feels as if it all comes back to him. "I put a man out of his misery."

"And let every person in that square know you were playing a zero sum game."

She's glad she's in a bed, on painkillers, and can't just wrap her hands around his neck. She schools her features as best she can. This isn't the time to show emotion. That will label her weak. Or feminine. All that old anger and grief he's dragged to the surface has to roil beneath still waters.

"Mr. Wisner, I appreciate your praise, but I hope you'll appreciate that I'm rather tired."

"Of course. Of course." He stands and picks up his hat from the end of her bed. "I'll let you get back to it." He looks as though he's leaving, but when he stops at the door, she knows it's a ruse. The conversation isn't over. "As I understand it, there was a girl involved."

"The spy?"

He shakes his head. "No, another one. A friend of yours?"

It's the way he says it. Casually. Easy to miss. But she can hear everything underneath and see Vince Pedrotti's sneer as he spat out the word "perverse."

"Friends are good. A lot of the men suited for this work have friends. The kind they can share secrets with. Teaches them how to keep a secret real well. But women?" He acts as though he has bad news, as if her stock portfolio has performed poorly. "Women don't get to have friends. They have friends or they have husbands." He slips his hat onto his head. "Do you understand, Miss Wright?"

This is the moment. This is the moment calling someone "perverse" makes sense. It's the moment the word—all the insinuation behind it—rankles and rips.

Her throat is so dry. Sore. Her voice a croak. "I do."

She doesn't scream.

She's in a hospital, and it wouldn't be appropriate.

And Amelia's waiting for her and will worry if she hears the scream from down the hall.

All Laura can do is smile congenially and bite the inside of her cheek.

Wisner leaves.

Seconds tick by, and Laura counts each one.

Amelia will come, and it will be okay. For just a little while, it will be okay.

Only Amelia never comes. The door doesn't open to reveal her, exasperated, worried, and glorious.

Michel comes instead. A lock of dark hair has fallen out of his carefully maintained coif and makes him look dashing. Covers his concern.

He almost hugs her, but Laura tenses, and he sees it. Instead, he settles into the chair Wisner used. He takes up less space and is a comfort where Wisner was a thorn.

"How are you feeling?"

"Asking about my headache or my guest?"

"Both?" His smile is sweet.

She looks to the ceiling so she doesn't have to consider it.

"There are plans to reform something like the OSS."

"That's good, yes?"

"Sure, but I was just told—"

Guileless. That's the word for Michel. Sweet and guileless and in love with her. He doesn't—shouldn't know about the ultimatum she received. It isn't fair to whine about her love life to a man so hopelessly wanting to be a part of it.

Wisner has made it clear. She has a choice. She can have the career she's hungry for or the woman she'd die for. Not both. Not now.

"Amelia's not here?"

The mention of her plainly irritates Michel. "No. Stole a car, left it in the middle of traffic and, according to some of the other young women at the hotel, she's currently in *Brooklyn*."

"She thinks I'm dead."

"As a doornail."

"The French are so charming."

"On occasion, we try."

Amelia's not here, and Laura's dead. A specter for Amelia to consider on dark nights. A chance flitting through her fingers.

It's easy then to ask a favor of Michel.

That's what she tells herself. *This* is easy. Amelia and a lot of other people think she's dead, and a war is just beginning that she could be a valuable soldier in. It's her duty.

She can disappear, and Amelia can do more than wait on the sidelines. She can have a chance of her own. At success. At happiness. Why court the disaster of what they both are when she can find joy?

And she can be safe.

That's what she tells herself.

Now, she just has to learn to believe it.

CHAPTER 13

S HE WATCHES THE FIRE BURN down to embers, and Laura never emerges. The firemen start cleaning up the scene, so she walks to the line of cabs taking the girls to a shelter and gives the driver her ma's address in Brooklyn instead.

Her ma's probably alarmed to have her daughter on her doorstep before dawn and smelling of smoke, but she just wraps her up in a firm hug and then takes her up the stairs to the bedroom Amelia used to share with her sister. Her sister's son sleeps in it now, but everyone insists it's okay for her to take the bed.

"He can sleep with us," her sister says, and she and her sleepy husband look as concerned as her ma. They're hugging their robes tight and watching all bleary-eyed.

Soon as her head hits the pillow—and it smells sour like a little kid—Amelia's out.

She doesn't dream. Or at least, she doesn't hold on to anything she can remember. Just closes her eyes and gets a few solid hours of nothingness. Which is a sight better than being homeless and sort of widowed.

Nah. She can't really call herself a widow. Can she? That implies a relationship that's longer than one night in the car and a few shared coffees at a diner.

Amelia's just… *alone*.

She mopes around in the kid's room. Lays on his bed and stares at the ceiling. It's painted over tin, and she counts each tile.

Downstairs, someone leans on the buzzer. She can hear the faint mumblings of a conversation before her nephew's heavy steps on the stairs.

"There's a man here to see you," he says. "Real fancy and French."

She goes down the stairs after him, the smell of smoke chasing her all the way.

Michel is standing in the middle of her ma's parlor, looking out of place in his expensive overcoat and polished shoes. He's got his hat in his hands, and his fingers fidget as if he wants to start twisting it between 'em.

"Can you guys leave us alone," she asks. She doesn't take her gaze off of him.

Her sister touches her shoulder on her way out. The whole family leaves and shuts the door after them.

It's a little funny. The door to the parlor's always supposed to stay open. "Ruins the airflow in the house." her ma's said on more than one occasion.

Last time it was closed, it was because her dad had to talk to Amelia about her funny and rotten feelings for other girls.

Boy she's glad he's dead and buried. Otherwise this whole affair would probably put him back in the ground again.

Michel sits on the sofa across from her and doesn't take off his coat.

"Found the car," he says. "The police called to say they'd impounded it after it was double parked half the night."

She shrugs and wishes she had something to drink. A nice soda that'd burn a little and be so sweet she wouldn't be able to think about anything else.

He scoots a little closer so that he's barely on the sofa. "I've just come from the hospital." He's real quiet, the way he says it. As if her family will hear and come storming in.

She tries not to get excited about him coming from the hospital. Tall, Dark, and French would have walked in happy if Laura were still alive. But he's all muted and concerned.

She doesn't say anything.

Man came all the way to Brooklyn to give her the bad news, and she's gonna make him do it without her help.

He tries pleading with those eyes of his. Sort of eyes that a girl's supposed to melt over.

Amelia just steels herself.

And waits.

Finally, Michel sighs, and the tears start prickling at the edge of Amelia's eyes. Softly, he says, "She was in the hotel when it burned down."

She knows. She was there. Felt the fire nearly blister her skin.

"I've come from the hospital where I... identified her body."

She doesn't cry, but the tears work backwards and burn like a knot of fury in her throat.

"I'm sorry."

That makes two of 'em.

He starts talking again. "I—" Stops. He gets more fidgety—more insufferable—by the minute. "I spoke to one of her colleagues."

"A spy."

He nods. "Apparently, her plan worked. Any suspicions someone might have had toward you—"

"Went up in flames."

He looks equal parts abashed and angry. "She cared about you, you know. Did all of this to keep you safe."

"Pretty steep cost, don't you think?"

"I'd agree."

Well… shit. Nice to know he blames her as much as she blames a dead woman.

"I'm… I'm sorry. That came out rudely."

"But it's honest." She sniffs and wipes the back of her hand across her nose. "More than I can say for most people."

He taps his finger on the brim of his hat. "I suppose. And this was Laura's choice, yes? She chose to sacrifice everything for you."

"Well aware. No need to rub it in."

"I only do so because…" He stands. "Because you should make it count, Miss Maldonado." He offers a handkerchief for the tears she didn't even notice were leaking down her cheeks.

Usually, the crying is supposed to stop all the pain in the throat, but this time it just makes it worse.

She glances at the clock over his shoulder and stands too. "I should go," she says, and Michel looks as surprised by the statement as she feels. "I've got an audition."

"Do you really think that's appropriate?"

The son of a bitch just told her to make Laura's death count—as if they were playing ball and she got herself out to set up a play. Now he's gotta question her?

"I'm homeless and heartbroken. Least I can do is get a good job."

She gets a great job.

She's reading her second scene, a big weepy one she's been working on for over a week. Her acting teacher has been telling her she's too showy with the scene. Telling her she needs to get "real." Whatever the hell that means.

Apparently, she figures out "real" up on stage under a single bare light. That knot in her throat loosens, and all her own grief pours out. The director, the casting girl, and even the producer stare at her with open mouths.

The producer mumbles. "She's like that Brando kid."

"Realism," the director says, unlit cigarette dangling from his lips.

She still has no idea what it means, but they offer her the role on the spot, and the pay is good enough that she scales back at the diner and can still afford a place that isn't her nephew's room at her Ma's house.

Everyone involved with the play tells her she's gonna be a star. They push her into interviews meant for the lead and try to book her on the radio. It's all so hurried, different, and new, and she forgets.

One day, she realizes it's been *two* days since she thought about Laura.

It happens to be at a Sunday family dinner when she's stepped out into the front garden for a smoke. She can see the family through the window, and they all look so happy. Picturesque. She's out between a tree and a lamppost, and there's a nice breeze making its way off the water a half mile away.

She thinks Laura would have liked it. She would have sat on the bench with her ankles crossed and leaned back to take a gander at the sky. Amelia would have stared at the long exposed expanse of Laura's neck, and it would have been just about the most content Amelia could have ever been.

She sits on the bench alone, and it's cold enough to send a chill up her backside.

Her uncle comes out after a while, and when he sits next to her it's with a little grunt. As if he's old, and the sitting on a hard concrete bench takes it out of him.

He lights his own cigar and offers her one wordlessly. He's never done that before. Cigars are supposed to be for the fellas.

But she puts out her cigarette and takes it. Lets him light it with a match. The flames flicker, and the skin of his hand has never looked so old.

They puff on their cigars in silence. Music from the house filters out, but it's too soft to hum to.

"I hear your play is going well."

"It's not going well until we open and get a few good reviews, but yeah, people seem excited."

"Your ma says it's the only thing you're cheerful about."

She tries to blow a smoke ring, but it comes out all wrong.

"I take it you haven't told her why you've been upset."

"And from this nice uncle act, I'm guessing you know?"

He nods. The smoke ring he blows is perfect. "I was sorry to hear it too."

She chuckles because she doesn't know what else to do. "Yeah," she says. "That makes two of us."

"You know, the day of the fire, she came by my house? Wanted me to 'protect' you. Insisted on it."

Cigars taste different than cigarettes. The smoke's heavier, and it settles around her head like a thick fog.

"I never really understood your… predilections, but that woman? She loved you enough that I don't think I have to."

Sort of like that knot in the back of her throat. Maybe it never left. Maybe it just grew a little looser every day until she learned to live with the ache.

But now, it's insistent and painful, and Amelia's hand flies to her mouth to keep it all in. Her uncle's arm comes around her shoulders and pulls her close, and the knot's so tight, it almost chokes her.

She cries, and it's hot and shameful and does nothing to fix the hurt.

"It's okay," her uncle says. He presses a gentle kiss to her temple. "You'll learn to live with it."

"When?"

She can see his ring on his finger. She never knew the woman he wears it for. "I'll tell you when I figure it out."

It'll never be okay.

Amelia learns to live with that knot.

But the night her play opens, they get a standing ovation, and she gets a cheer bigger than the leads. They smile and pull her forward to bask in the glow of all that praise.

She can't see much with the lights shining in her eyes, but she thinks she sees Laura in the back of the crowd. Smiling as if she never died. Beaming with pride that's balanced only by the melancholy of distance.

And Amelia bows, and when she rights herself the visage is gone.

The knot in her throat doesn't hurt so bad.

The knot in her throat never leaves.

CHAPTER 14

SIX YEARS LATER

AMELIA'S SITTING ON A BENCH that cost more than a month's rent at the Sebastian and staring into a mirror with an honest-to-God gilded frame. Her hair's done up. Years on Broadway has her able to do a twist without thinking.

Classy. That's what the rags call it. Especially paired with all the pearls and sapphires and satin gowns.

Classy Amelia Maldonado. Only they don't call her that anymore.

She got the call from Hollywood, and the suits—dressed just as fancy as those fellows who'd once tried to kill her— told her to lighten her hair and wear more powder to cover her "tan" and change her name to something less "ethnic." She thought of Laura again. All WASP and reserved and a "right bastard" if ever there was one.

"Amelia Wright," she said immediately.

So now, she is Amelia Wright, and she's getting ready for a big movie premiere. Her first since that Oscar three months ago.

Someone knocks on the door. It's Tab, the good looking kid they said she needs on her arm for the premiere.

"People will talk," her agent said very politely.

"They'll think you're queer," the studio suit said, not so politely.

So, she steps out into the hall of the hotel with Tab on her arm and smiles.

"You ready, Miss Wright?"

After pistols and tommy guns aimed at her head, flash bulbs and screaming fans are a piece of cake. Amelia walks the red carpet real smooth, signing autographs and gamely tackling questions.

The epitome of grace.

Until she sees a face in the crowd. Standing in a throng of teens and housewives. Red dress that brings out the brassiness of her blonde hair and pairs like a good wine with the unfashionable tan on her skin. Red lips, too. Painted red lips curled up into a smile.

Laura.

She shakes her head. Focuses on the person with the pen and pad in front of her. Someone asks when she and Tab are getting married. He blushes, and she laughs.

It's a cultured laugh.

She learned that when she came to Hollywood. "This isn't the sticks." As if Broadway and her Tony award were all done in some barn in Pennsylvania. "It's the real thing, Wright. So laugh again."

She did. She laughed. She cried. She worked with diction coaches who worked the New York out of her like wrinkles in a dress.

A fan thrusts an autograph pad in her face, and she signs. Again, she sees Laura, this time talking to a cop at the edge of the red carpet.

Again Amelia shakes her head.

"Maybe," she says to the next kid who asks if she's getting married.

At the end of the red carpet, Laura—who can't be there— smiles as if she heard what Amelia said.

Tab takes her by the elbow. "You okay," he asks. His breath smells like cigarettes.

"Fine."

"We're almost through." He has to lean down to say it into her ear. Can't let the cameras catch it. They can read lips if they want to.

America's embroiled in a non-war with the USSR, and it'd be done in half a day if they put entertainment rags on the case.

They go inside, and there she is again, climbing the staircase. No one else must see her. No one's saying anything. No one's gasping and pointing.

"There's a lady war hero!"

"A spy!"

"Supposed to be dead!"

"She went down on Amelia Wright for twenty minutes and didn't even stop for air!"

Nothing.

As if Laura's a ghost. Haunting Amelia all alone.

Someone takes her hand and pumps it up and down as if water's gonna spout out of her mouth, and she has to smile and be gracious.

The way to their seats takes at least an hour. There's pause after pause. Smiles and jokes and never letting her voice get too loud. They don't like it when she's loud. "Makes you sound coarse."

She'll show 'em coarse.

Tab smiles, too.

And glances at her.

A lot.

Usually when she *thinks* she sees Laura moving through the crowd.

When they're finally settling into their seats, he speaks to her, his voice is real low. "What's going on with you?"

"That new war picture they're hot to have me in."

"That French Resistance flick," he asks, surprised. "That's what you're thinking about?"

It's gotta be.

Now that she's said it, it makes sense.

They want her playing a gross caricature of a woman she loved. So, she's seeing her ghost.

Some kind of guilt thing.

Like a heart beatin' under the floorboards.

"It's an awful script," she says.

"But this one's good, right?" He means the premiere. It's a western. Her obligatory one.

"Yeah." She pats his knee and smiles.

A quarter of the way through the movie, someone starts coughing, and it isn't the good kind.

The good kind is phlegm. It's something in the throat, trying to get out.

This is the fake kind that rankles her as bad as talking while she's up on the stage.

She tries to ignore it.

Fidgets.

Bounces.

Finally, she turns to tell the cougher to shove it where the sun don't shine.

Laura grins, hand falling away from her lips—which are still red as sin. The people around her are glaring as if she's Satan, but Laura is definitely smiling just for her.

So Amelia turns around and tries to watch the movie.

Up on screen, she's covered in dust and chasing after Stewart Granger as he goes off to slaughter someone in order to save her life. They can't be together, though.

They think they're brother and sister.

She'd hoot about how awful it all is, but a ghost just razzed her movie by coughing.

So, she stares real hard at the screen. Her dress is too tight, and she wonders how they got it past the censors. She's pretty sure, if she squints, she can see the outline of a nipple.

Behind her, people grumble, and there's shuffling and rustling.

When she glances back again, Laura's seat is empty.

She's not gonna say she's frantic, but Amelia does look hurriedly around the rest of the theater until—there. The ghost is standing at the exit and staring straight through Amelia as if she's made of glass.

She gulps and turns back around.

Waits.

Stewart Granger's been hurt, and she's got his head in her lap, stroking his hair.

"Excuse me," she says to Tab.

He's confused when she has to swish past. So's the director. And the suits. And Stewart.

"You should use the little-ladies' room before you come," Stewart says as she slides past him.

She moves quickly toward the exit, bottom of her dress in her hands, head down.

No one mumbles or mutters. As bad as the film is—and it's a doozy—it's still entertaining.

The lobby is less entertaining. It's empty.

Not even an usher with a flashlight.

A door closes somewhere, so she heads toward the noise.

Of course. The women's restroom.

Only inside is empty. No Laura. No one looking to relieve herself. Not even a bathroom attendant. She walks all the way through to be sure. Even peers under the doors like a creep. Nothing.

Which is how she finds herself looking into another mirror. Glaring at her own damn face. She leans on the sink and tries to get her bearings.

It's got to be the stupid war movie. It's got her thinking about a woman dead since forty-six. She's got Laura on the mind.

She turns on the faucet and stares at the water.

Wouldn't be good to splash her face. Her makeup would run, and people would talk.

She laughs.

God, she's going crazy.

She pulls water into her hands and sips it.

Completely nuts.

She sniffs.

Aw jeeze.

She's gonna cry. She can feel it.

It's the stupid knot in the back of her throat. It's gotten to be a comfort. A pain she relishes on lonely nights.

Now it's got her about to cry.

Big crazy tears that'll get her carted off to the loony bin. She tries to laugh it off, and that makes the threat of sobs even worse.

The door opens, and she straightens up and schools her face into something neutral. "Sorry," she immediately says. "I just had a..."

"Successful film premiere by the looks of it."

Laura smiles as if she's not dead. When she steps closer, her heels clack on the tile like real heels. Her red dress is tasteful up close. All of her is. Hair down. Makeup perfect.

Older.

Because time isn't gonna wait around.

But Laura.

A sob bursts out of Amelia, and she has to cover her mouth.

"I believe," Laura's real careful, as if Amelia's a skittish animal, "you once likened us to a disaster. Which makes sense. Our careers. Our 'proclivities.' Disastrous." There's that smirk of Laura's that will always do things to the inside of Amelia.

She mutters between her fingers. "End of the world." She's not quite sure she's existing in reality.

"When I left, I had hoped it would keep you safe. And I wanted...I didn't want a disaster."

"Good for you."

It must sting, because Laura winces. "But I've...I've lived a life that's more appropriate for my line of work, and I've watched you be extraordinary and..."

Amelia takes a step toward her. "What?"

She shrugs. "A world I can't share with you is miserable."

"Yeah. I know."

"And I'm tired of being miserable." Laura's not the only one.

"So what then?"

It's that crooked smile.

"End the world with me, Amelia Maldonado?"

CHAPTER 15

H E IS A DEAR MAN, and Laura loves her children. Their home is very nice, and the neighborhood is very beautiful.

But she is positively, irritatingly, bored.

Michel sits across from her reading the paper. He looks up. Smiles. Sips his juice.

Laura is just utterly bored.

"Exciting day," he asks.

Work discussions can be... trying sometimes. She works as an agent for one of the fastest growing intelligence agencies in the world and regularly travels across said world to shiv enemy agents. He's a diplomat and spends his evenings in white tie and tails, dining with other diplomats. The jobs aren't comparable.

At his dinner parties, everyone assumes she's a nice girl from Connecticut, happy to be the diplomat's wife who spends her days raising their children—with the aid of a lovely nanny, of course. At *her*—rare—dinner parties, people talk to Michel slowly. As if he is simple.

So, in addition to being bored, Laura is also, perhaps, wrapped up in a marriage full of contentiousness.

They do sleep in separate beds, after all.

She smiles at her husband and sips her tea. "Lovely, I hope."

He nods. Tilts his head. Continues drinking his juice as he stares at his paper. "Hey, you used to know this one, yes?"

He turns the newspaper around to show her a picture of a stunning woman who was always rather addictively ordinary, but never ever boring. Amelia Maldonado.

Last name's different now.

Because she's changed. She's not the girl working at the diner, going over her lines in a mutter, and beating on Laura's door for late night gab sessions.

Now she's Amelia—

Amelia Wright.

Her new film is premiering in New York, and according to the headline, people are anticipating the announcement of a proposal. *Could it Be Love* is splayed over the top of the photo. Apparently, much of the country wants Amelia to marry some idiot actor named Tab.

Oh. She squints. There is actually a bland-looking, skinny boy in a tux standing by Amelia.

It makes something unexpected clinch up inside of Laura.

Which isn't fair. Amelia is free to live her life however she chooses. Laura gave up any right to comment when she let Amelia think she was dead.

"You remember her?" Laura is surprised by Michel's question.

"How could I forget you drugging a girl and leaving her on my father's couch?"

"She had more gumption than sense."

"And you fiercely told her you wouldn't lose anyone else." He says it evenly. There's no frustration there—even though Michel can clearly guess why she cared so deeply.

They've very carefully never discussed it.

She dips her ridged spoon into the flesh of the grapefruit in front of her. Eats sans sugar. The tartness claws at her tongue and tries to draw her cheeks together.

She says simply, "She was the first friend I had after the war. I wasn't about to have her killed."

She takes the paper from him and studies Amelia. She's done away with the girlish curls she wore when Laura knew her. Her hair is sleek and styled. In the photo, it's in a twist. No doubt to show off the expensive earrings and necklace she's wearing.

But.

But Amelia doesn't look happy. Laura can see that. She's a spy. Her training—her very life—is devoted to reading other people. So she can look at this innocent picture of Amelia Maldonado and know beyond any shadow of a doubt that Amelia is not happy.

"I was very fond of her."

Michel looks sympathetic. "She still thinks you're..."

She nods. "A necessity."

They can't discuss it further. Amelia is like Michel's brother. A topic better danced around. Besides, their nanny is walking in with the twins in tow, and she thinks Laura's a dilettante homemaker.

Laura snaps the newspaper into a fold and hands it back. She kisses her children good-bye, gives her husband a peck on the cheek and makes her way to the bus stop.

Wife of a diplomat, and she has to take two buses to get to work. Wouldn't do to use her husband's driver, or her own car. No Laura Wright has to be a very different woman down in Foggy Bottom.

Quiet.

Polite.

She has to be fond of beige suits and peering at maps and fetching coffee and files. And waiting for the under-the-table assignments that only she and Frank Wisner know about. "That's your cover," he told her with a grin. "If you're the meek little analyst and coffee girl, then no one will blink when I send you to Guatemala or Greece."

It works marvelously, but the majority of her day tends toward excruciatingly boring.

For half of this particular day, she stares out the window at the fog resting lightly on the Potomac. She taps the tip of her pen against her chin and tries not to think about Amelia Maldonado.

Normally, that isn't so hard. She has children she cares a great deal for, a job that often consumes her, and a husband who…Well, she's fond of him.

"How about friends?" he asked when she confessed that she'd had enough great loves in her life and wasn't about to add him to the list. "Friends who make a life together?"

Sometimes, she pities her husband. It must be hard living in the shadow of a dead man and sharing a home with a woman who is very much in love with another woman.

One she hasn't spoken to since 1946.

They've a new president now. And Laura's an agent again. And Amelia has an Oscar.

And a Tony.

And fans. Whole legions of them.

She certainly doesn't need one more.

In her section's office, there's a whole slew of televisions on one wall. They play broadcasts from all over the country. Piping them in and displaying them in fuzzy black and white. It's a costly investment. One the general balked at, but his second, Dulles, was all too eager to indulge for his favorite employee, Frank Wisner.

"I've seen a few of his skeletons," Wisner said when Laura once pressed him about it. Then he gulped his beer like a cowboy in Colorado. "The trick is to know all their secrets and make sure you have none of your own."

A swath of grayscale passes along one screen, and Laura has to stand and move closer. Sometimes, from her desk, it's too hard to make out who's on screen.

She looms over the TV sets, hands wrapped around her middle, fingers digging into her side.

Because there's Amelia again. This time, it's a movie. That dreadful domestic drama that won her an Academy Award.

"Hey Wright, you getting paid to watch flicks," someone asks.

Someone else chuckles. Makes some comment about the flightiness of her "sex."

"Shove it," she barks, eyes still on the screen.

Amelia looks radiant—if fuzzy. She's just light hitting electrons. A ghost of physics scattered against the glass.

Not the real thing. A woman who was warm against Laura's lips, pliant beneath her fingers as she sighed into Laura's hair and came against her hand.

A woman who took on the mob to save her and laughed at Laura's bad jokes and… cared.

A woman who loved her.

A woman Laura abandoned for a job she only gets to do half the time.

She rounds on the other analysts in the room—the clever women just doing their jobs and the idiot men always angling to tease.

The "good-natured" ribbing stops.

Her heels are loud on the brown tiles as she stalks back to her desk and snatches up her purse.

She feels the need to have a secret. And damn Frank Wisner to hell if he protests.

On occasion, by people who Laura has only a passing fondness for, she's been called "impulsive."

Her father's said it more than once. Usually after she beat the snot out of a bully in an effort to protect the bullied. "Just because it's right," he'd say with a sigh, "doesn't mean you ought to run off and do it."

Standing in a bathroom at Radio City Music Hall, decked out in an evening gown and far from the family she made a go at forging, she can hear father's admonishment in her head.

She's not wrong in this instance.

Staring at a flesh and blood Amelia poised over a sink, trying to collect herself, Laura knows, beyond the shadow of a doubt, she's being impulsive.

But she speaks up anyways.

Amelia seems to be crying and apologizing for it, as if she's done something wrong. "Sorry. I just had a…"

"Successful film premiere by the looks of it." Laura's impulsive, but she's also very suave. She once broke a soldier's mind with nothing more than a smile and a nice dress.

Amelia looks confused.

That's a natural response. Particularly for a girl who was once drugged and abandoned by a woman who then faked her own death.

So, Laura decides to fill in the blanks. She approaches Amelia carefully and tells her how wonderful her career appears to be. How she's so proud. How she's so madly in l—

The crack of Amelia's palm against Laura's face is so loud, she's surprised cops don't burst in with guns blazing.

"You fake your death and disappear for six years, and now you want to end the world with me?"

Now that Amelia's spitting her words back at her incredulously, Laura has to admit they sound… silly.

"Ya think?" It's all South Brooklyn that comes dripping off Amelia's tongue.

"Oh! Your accent. I thought you lost it."

She's so formal and breathy in her pictures.

Amelia slaps her again. This time with the other hand.

Laura rounds on her and suspects she looks upset. "Are you quite finished?"

"I don't know, Laura. I still haven't socked you in the mouth." She balls her small fist up for emphasis.

"I'll take the slap thanks."

"I just—I can't believe you! The gall. And the chutzpah. And the gall." She lightly punches Laura now. But in the shoulder. "Showing up looking like that. Smiling! At my premiere?"

"I had hoped..." She sighs. "I had hoped it would be romantic?"

Amelia gives her the stink eye—something she hasn't experienced in years. Spies tend to not give one another the stink eye. It's gauche.

She's immediately grateful this meeting is private, because otherwise she might be a smidge embarrassed.

"Tell me something, Laura, if some gorgeous dame had gone and wooed you in a spectacular fashion, genuinely connected with you on an emotional level, and then drugged you, locked you up in a mansion 'for your own good,' and faked her death, how would you feel?"

She'd have punched her into the next decade.

"Right. So how do you think I feel? Particularly when I can't help but notice that set of rings gleaming on your finger."

She glances down. Shit. "I'd... meant to remove those."

Amelia crosses her arms. "Not helping."

"Amelia," Laura says, distracted when Amelia sighs. She's quickly getting fed up with Laura. So Laura has to forge ahead. "Have you ever felt just—just an all consuming need to see someone. To be with someone?"

Amelia swallows as she stares.

Perhaps it's working? Laura comes closer. "You... you're who I need."

She's close enough now, she could kiss Amelia if she didn't think she'd get punched for the attempt.

Amelia glares up at her, lower lip stuck out. She looks more like herself than all the glamour and sophistication that she's become as Amelia Wright.

"Then maybe you shouldn't have left me and gone and gotten married."

Well. That will knock the wind out of anyone's sails.

She pushes past Laura, their shoulders touching as she does. It's supposed to be a brush off. A good-bye. Sayonara. Do svidanyia.

But they both gasp at the contact, as if there's something electric there.

And Amelia stops. They're shoulder to shoulder. Facing opposite directions. Her hand, wrapped in a satin glove, is centimeters from Laura's own.

Laura just has to curl her fingers, and they're around Amelia's hand.

She doesn't look at her. It's as if one of them is Veronica Lake, casting a spell in that ridiculous witch movie. Looking at one another will break the spell and usher in the wretched feelings that rightfully consume Amelia and have deftly dodged Laura.

Amelia's sharp intake of breath at the contact, though, *that* sorely tempts Laura. Her whole body thrums with potent need.

"I'm sorry." And she is. She's so, so sorry.

Amelia's fingers, ever so delicately, brush against Laura's. She can hear the scrape of satin sliding over her skin. Then Amelia sighs, and her hand falls away, leaving Laura impossibly cold. "You're married and I'm—"

"Engaged?"

She laughs. This gorgeous, sultry laugh. Much throatier than anything she'd do in one of her pictures.

"Whatever you're looking for in New York isn't here, Laura. So how about you go back to your happy life and just think of me as that twit up on the screen."

"We both know that's impossible."

"Maybe. But it's a necessity too. Isn't it?"

There's a whisper of cloth, and Amelia is standing in front of her again, so close she might feel the heat of her. She presses her satin-clad hand against Laura's cheek. "We're a disaster remember?" The corner of her mouth crooks up. "So how about we avoid the apocalypse?"

She reaches up to wrap her hand around Amelia's and takes another step toward her. Amelia doesn't back down. She's not the sort. So, they're impossibly, irritatingly, close to one another. "I told you, I'd much rather end the world with you."

That earns her a genuine smile. The kind Amelia used to dole out like the government gives milk for children. "Anyone ever tell you, you talk too much?"

Amelia speaks softly. Intimately. And Laura feels obliged to do the same. She doesn't bother to hide the small smile growing. "Not in quite some time."

She very much wants to cross that small distance and press her lips to Amelia's. It would be simple, and it feels right, and Laura is even doing it—her eyes drifting closed.

But she's stopped by Amelia, who suddenly darts forward and kisses the corner of her mouth. "See ya, Laura."

Then she's out of the room in a quick flurry of satin and silk and exorbitantly priced perfume.

CHAPTER 16

LAURA WASN'T RAISED IN A military setting. Her father served, yes, but he was more a lawyer than a soldier, and her mother was as stalwart a pacifist as ever lived. All the rigid routine and necessity for rigorous planning wasn't a natural impulse for Laura or some chief component of her upbringing.

This is made obvious by her idiot move of driving to New York City to confess her love in the middle of a movie premiere.

But Laura has to admit, sometimes there is merit to the military's love for planning.

Case in point, the Amelia Maldonado affair.

If Laura had planned it like an op, it might have ended in sighing, kissing, and twelve straight hours of sex in a hotel room.

So, round two she plans as if it's an op, only with less scouring of maps and anticipation of fatalities. She really wants Operation Woo Amelia to go off without a few murders.

Step one of her new op is the simplest one. Laura calls a friend in Truman's office and asks if one Amelia Wright is on the list to perform at the White House Correspondents' Dinner.

Why no, she is not.

Oh? Really? Well, if it isn't too much trouble, you should ask her. She sings wonderfully, and this new western has made her quite popular with your boss's constituents.

"Oh, thank you so much for the suggestion, ma'am!"

If Amelia will accept the offer, she will then have to be in Washington, DC, a considerably smaller town than New York. So if she and Laura "happen" to run into one another, it could be a coincidence. The sort that Laura can smoothly play off as a surprise.

Which is exactly what she does when she "runs into" Amelia at the White House a week and a half later. Amelia's just met the President and First Lady and enjoyed a tour of the reconstruction of the White House. She's wearing a Christian Dior suit and daringly shaped hat, making her easily the most stylish woman in a twelve-block radius.

Laura is wearing her favorite pinstripe gray suit, and until she saw Amelia, she was sure *she* was the most stylish woman in a twelve-block radius. Now she's excited and envious and also on her way to meet with the President's cabinet on matters of world security.

They see each other. Laura smiles so widely her cheeks hurt. Amelia looks startled. Glances away.

Not one to be dissuaded, Laura smoothly steps in front of her. "Miss Wright, I'm a tremendous fan of your work," she announces enthusiastically. It's odd saying her own name like that.

Amelia peers at her for a moment, as if she's trying to figure out Laura's game. Something softens around her eyes, and she dryly says, "Thanks."

"Were you...Were you looking for the bathroom? I can escort you." It's a terrible excuse. So bad, in fact, that she has to take Amelia's hand and guide her toward a bathroom before her escort, a clean-cut teen in a blue suit and White House tie, can protest or Amelia herself can point out how lousy the excuse is.

The bathroom is empty. There's two stalls, and both doors are wide open. Laura leans against the door, and its handle digs into the small of her back. She tries to be as suave as humanly possible. "We've got to stop meeting like this."

It's the second time they've met in a bathroom in as many weeks.

It's very funny.

Amelia isn't as amused. In fact, she seems a little more nervous. She tugs at her gloves and then pulls down the bottom of her jacket. "What on earth are you doing here?" She fidgets with her hat.

"Meeting with the President."

She shakes her head. "You're pulling my leg."

"I'm not. In fact I will now be," she glances at her watch, "two minutes late." Dulles and Wisner will kill her.

"Then maybe you better skedaddle?" Amelia is clearly, impossibly, confused. And her hat is off-kilter. It's endearing.

"I will. I am." She takes a step toward Amelia, her sensible heels clacking on the tile, and Amelia steps back, her more sophisticated shoes barely making a sound. "I just wanted to apologize. The other day I made a tit... of us both."

Amelia's so very even. She stares, her sharp brown eyes unblinking and focused on somewhere around Laura's nose. "Real tit."

"I should have been more... delicate."

"A little."

"And I understand if you're not keen on—if you're not keen on me. But I would like to hope we could be friends?"

She laughs. Did Amelia always have that sort of laugh or was it something cultivated out west? "Laura, whatever we are, it isn't friends."

Laura sighs.

"And whatever we may be? It's not gonna be fair to the fella whose rings you're wearing."

Reflexively, Laura's thumb brushes across her rings. She really should take them off. "What if I told you we were getting a divorce?" Laura sounds too hopeful about it for polite company.

Amelia smirks, "I'd say that was some timing."

There's a half dozen other things Laura can say then. Though they're all likely to go as well as this current exchange. "Well. Then." She slaps the files in her hand against her thigh. "I'm sorry for wasting your time." She glances at herself in the mirror, then at Amelia, who stares so hard when she thinks Laura isn't looking. "I suppose we should go look for your escort now?"

"Sounds like a plan."

She holds the door for Amelia and guides her out. Her tour guide is at the other end of the hall looking deeply confused.

"Hey, Laura," Amelia says, smile bright and eyes on anything but Laura. "You know a Representative Chalmers?"

She does. He's on the Foreign Affairs committee and a frequent guest at the dinner parties Michel hosts.

He's insufferable.

"We met at a party a few months ago, and he's just been absolutely delighted I'm in town," Amelia says conversationally. She pushes at her hat again and tries to fix it. Laura probably should have given her time to use the mirror. "Keeps taking me out to dinner."

Laura plasters on her biggest and falsest smile. "How lovely."

Amelia's eyes flicker over her, and Laura thinks, that maybe, she kind of smiles. Like she's being put on. "Apparently, he's got a big dinner party he's going to in a couple of days. Would just love for me to join him."

It is only through considerable grace and willpower that Laura doesn't trip. "Are you... attending?"

"Sounds as if it could be a hoot. I'm just glad I have a date." They're almost to her escort, and Amelia turns and takes Laura's hand in hers and squeezes it as if they're old school friends. She's smiling so brightly Laura wishes she'd worn her sunglasses inside. "Would be a little funny if I showed up all alone, huh?"

She smiles back. "Yes. Yes, I suppose it would," Laura says congenially.

Files stowed under her arm, Laura reaches up and rights Amelia's hat.

And Amelia swoops in and kisses her cheek. It's all very friendly, things women who happen to be friends do. "Next time, just send me an invitation," she murmurs, her lips feather light against Laura's ear.

Laura would be inclined to agree, but she's busy being something of a tit again. It's Amelia's proximity. And her voice. And the way she's cottoned on to Laura's plan.

Unlike some people, Amelia Maldonado is never boring.

"I wasn't sure you'd attend," she manages to croak.

"That makes two of us."

That night, she comes home a little later than usual, and Michel is in the kitchen staring hard at a peculiar arrangement of flowers. They're shaped like a bird.

"Where on earth did these come from," she asks.

Michel doesn't saying anything. Just hands her the card as he continues to stare. It is very uncommon to get something like a foot-and-a-half-tall arrangement of flowers shaped like a bird.

There's no signature. Just a neat scrawl that Laura remembers well from the checks at a New York City diner once upon a time.

How about, from now on, this be the only tit in the room.

Laura snorts so loudly it wakes the children.

CHAPTER 17

MICHEL HIRES A PIANIST FOR the dinner party. A young American prodigy with a shock of blond curls sprouting from the top of his head. He sits at the piano, churning out Russian concertos with swaggering flourishes. Everyone lingers in the drawing room to listen and murmur quietly around him as they sip their rum tonics and gin fizzes.

Laura is ordinarily a good hostess, but tonight she sips her own bourbon on the rocks too often and glances at the door. One shoe dangles on her toe and the heel wags, and Michel sometimes squints at her as if he thinks staring will explain her nerves.

He's the only one to notice though. Laura is, if nothing else, a professional spy. She can hide the nerves from everyone but him.

And maybe Amelia.

Who isn't there. And isn't there. And isn't there.

Until she is.

The bell rings forty minutes after the party's started and twenty minutes before the meal is served. She smiles and smooths the skirt of her dress down. There's no need to announce that she'll get it.

She's the hostess and always answers the door.

Chalmers's bulk takes up too much of the doorway. His tuxedo stretches across a broad chest and broader shoulders.

"Mrs. Sauveterre," he says. His voice oil on all her water.

Her smile is tight. "Representative Chalmers. How lovely."

"Sorry I am so late. My date doesn't believe in clocks."

His date is standing just behind him and looks as peeved as Laura feels. In fact, when she catches Laura's glance, she rolls her eyes and makes a face. One that quickly disappears when he turns around to introduce her.

"Laura Sauveterre, this is Amelia Wright, the actress."

He says it significantly. As if Amelia might be fine Italian leather or a rare wine he procured.

Amelia smiles. "Why Laura, it's been ages." Her voice is high and bright, and Laura leans into the kiss pressed to her cheek. "Mike, dear, didn't I tell you? Laura and I go way back."

"An absolute distance," she agrees.

"Good! Good. You two can catch up while the rest of us chat. Now, darling, can you point me toward your husband?" he says.

She nods back toward the piano music, which has turned into something jazzy. "The drawing room, just past the gin."

Amelia waits for Chalmers to disappear around the corner before stepping in. She seems shy, with her purse held in front of her, and her head ducked down. "Bit of a step up from the Sebastian, huh?"

"No, Mrs. Myrtle is a considerable improvement."

She hands Laura her stole and deposits her gloves in her purse before handing it over too. "Bet it's a lot easier to sneak in and out."

"I know Michel in particular misses the old place. He was rather fond of devising ways to sneak in, and here he just has to use the front door."

There's something sharp in Amelia's bright eyes. "Are you and Michel still... friends?"

"Married," she says and tries to ignore the glare boring into the back of her skull.

"Now I know why my invitation must have gotten lost. Do they all know what you two do—did?"

Laura hangs Amelia's things in the front closet and keeps her voice low. "Sadly, no. Michel's a mere diplomat now, and I'm a simple housewife or something equally banal to the people in the other room."

"Darning socks?"

"And obsessing over soap operas. I think I'm supposed to be curious about *Guiding Light*," she mockingly drops a hand to her chest, "but am remaining loyal to *Search for Tomorrow*."

"See, I'm a *Love of Life* girl myself. Need something short and sweet, you know? Can't be weighed down by all that time." Amelia's words dance on a razor.

When they step into the drawing room, the young boy playing piano stops and stares in awe. Others turn too and Chalmers's barrel chest puffs out. "Ah dear, I was beginning to think you'd gotten lost." He holds his hand out for Amelia, and she obliges.

Laura pours herself another drink and watches the party fawn over the latest guest. Their faces are all flushed with eagerness and a little envy and lust, and Chalmers puts his arm around Amelia's shoulders as if he's got a right to.

But Amelia.

She has this grace Laura never would have thought her to have. This kind of goddess come down from the mountain to move amongst the mortals. Laura wraps one arm around herself, sips her drink, and basks in Amelia.

It has to be like this. They must stay apart... all of the time. Yet Amelia's swanning through her party, and Laura is again completely enamored.

So enamored it takes her a moment to realize Michel is glaring at her from across the room. Genuinely glaring too. When he finally catches her eye, he tilts his head in Amelia's direction, and Laura has to smile and shrug.

He doesn't relax when they are all seated for dinner—the prodigy now playing some sweet bit of Chopin—and Amelia mentions that she and Laura were neighbors back in New York "after the war."

"Have you kept up?" Wallis's wife asks.

"Not since the Sebastian burned down," Amelia says. "I didn't even realize she'd gotten married."

Amelia's bright eyes fall on Laura's rings, and then they're dancing around the table, settling on each person that speaks. She's got a way about her—one she's always had—where she can make anyone feel as if they are the center of her world. It was something that used to enchant Laura.

Now, it infuriates her a little. Makes her feel used. A little less special.

What an awful thing...

After dinner, they gather again, and Chalmers leans back in a chair Laura likes to read in and rests a hand on the small of Amelia's back and tells her to sing.

It isn't an order, but it rankles Laura as such.

Others chime in, and Amelia smiles in that charming way of someone who's very good at what she does and is about to show off.

She crosses the room and hip checks the prodigy, who smiles boyishly. "What'll we wow them with," she asks him in a conspiratorial stage whisper.

He wags his eyebrows and the two of them are off. Speaking in a secret language of musicians. "This one?" he says and follows it with a flourish on the keys.

"No that one." And then Amelia leans over and taps a few more.

Back and forth playfully until it becomes a song itself. Unfamiliar.

Then familiar. A true song plays. Some standard from the late thirties when Laura drifted through music halls in a haze of booze and excitement. It's a playful song about a woman who knows a man doesn't love her. People smile, and Chalmers laughs, and Laura tries not to flush with ill-conceived embarrassment.

The song isn't about her, and she knows it. The way Amelia grins, she knows it too. She's teasing. Flirting. When she spies Laura through the throng, lips finally tilted up into a smile, she looks completely sated.

The song's not about her, but now it's a joke. One just between the two of them. Mute laughter alighting across the room like candlelight on crystal.

For a moment, the others in the room are just refractions. Shadows. Gone.

For a moment, if Amelia sighed, it would be for Laura's ears alone.

The prodigy's playing slows and twists and turns, and then half the room groans because apparently he's moved onto some popular—and hokey—Broadway tune. Amelia chuckles and sings along, telling the whole world how they kiss in shadows.

Her eyes catch Laura's again, and Laura has to lean against the wall and cross her legs at the ankle. It's as if hot fire pools inside and spreads out from the center of her.

But then there's cold water in the form of small feet thumping almost silently on the stairs. She peeks around the corner and sees her daughter and son pressed against the wall, listening. They are as enchanted by Amelia's voice as their mother.

When they see her, they blanch, only to calm when she brings her finger to her lips and winks.

They all listen together.

Over on his chair, even Michel bobs his head a little.

But eventually the spell releases its hold, and Amelia is bowing out from a full concert and the prodigy is playing something borderline ribald that has half the room in tears.

Laura motions to her children to sneak back upstairs, but Wallis sees them first. They are both trucked out in a fashion to smile and bow and curtsy for the room. Amelia's eyes are wide and waifish at the sight of them.

"I didn't know you had children," she says, her voice hoarse.

One of the children declares they're twins, and the other hoots agreement. The party all laughs, except for Amelia who is still looking at Laura's children with wide wet eyes.

Then Laura insists they go to bed and announces she'll see them up herself. She suffers the little looks of delight and sympathy the rest of the room shoots her.

"You've got a good wife there, Sauveterre," Chalmers declares.

She's so very good about resisting the urge to beat him to death with the silver platter on the buffet. She makes a point not to look at Amelia as she goes. Being the good little wife is humiliating enough without having to see Amelia's look of pity.

Upstairs she's feeling indulgent and a little giddy and reads her children a story. They can both read a little on their own, but they're young enough to like hearing about Babar the elephant from their mother.

A creak sounds in the hall, and Laura knows they're not alone. Someone—not her husband—has come to watch her read. Michel's walk is distinctive. No, this person is wearing heels and moves with a shuffle of delicate and expensive fabric. Even before she looks over her shoulder and finds her leaning against the door frame, she's sure it's Amelia.

She watches them with dark eyes and has a ghost of what could be a smile on her lips. All Laura can do is smile back.

When the children realize they have a guest, they brighten considerably. The parties never migrate into their bedroom, and this is cause for celebration. Her daughter recognizes Amelia first and then reminds her brother who she is. They beg for her to finish the tale their mum's begun.

"You're an actress," her son says breathlessly. Her daughter nods eagerly, and Laura is forced to give up her seat and book to the more appropriate storyteller.

Amelia comes from a sizable family, and Laura has it on good authority that she's aunt to many nieces and nephews. Reading a children's book is little more than an acting exercise to her. But Laura watches raptly all the same. Watches the way Amelia engages with the children, eyes shining in the glow of the little pink lamp. Watches the way she uses her hands and modulates her tone. Watches as her fingers flick through the pages, rattling the bracelet on her wrist.

Amelia is happily occupied by Laura's children. She's buoyant, and Laura wants to join in—but the scene is so close to one consigned only to idle daydreams. So she can do nothing more than watch and enjoy the warmth unfurling inside of her.

"Oscar caliber," she says quietly when the children are near passed out and Amelia has come to the close of the story.

"Definitely going on my reel," Amelia jokes. She hands the book to Laura, and Laura kneels and puts it away.

When she rises again Amelia's closer, but her smile's gone. It's been replaced with something intoxicatingly enigmatic.

Laura nods toward the direction of the hall, and they exit the bedroom. She dims the lights and closes the door as she goes.

Amelia holds her hands behind her, and she speaks softly, demurely. "You've got two wonderful children."

There's so much there, and some of it frightens Laura.

"Thank you. I am rather fond of them."

Amelia makes a show of looking around the hallway. "And a lovely home."

Laura agrees. Steps closer.

Amelia steps back, stopping when her hands and hips brush the console table right behind her. She looks up at Laura who is so close she can smell more of Amelia than just her perfume.

Her breath is a whisper across Laura's lips.

"It seems rather perfect."

She notes that Amelia makes no mention of the husband downstairs.

Good.

"Not quite." She tries not to look at all of Amelia, to not look at her lips. She fails miserably.

Amelia, though, Amelia's staring her in the eye, demanding her attention in the way only generals ever could. "What's missing?"

Laura's hands find their way to the console table, bringing her close enough that their hips could touch if they like. She's trapped Amelia in, but she's the one that feels caught. She swallows. "You know." Her voice is hoarse.

As much as she desires it, as much as she feels the need, she will not kiss Amelia. Not now. Amelia's made it clear. All she's allowed to do is be there, taking up all the space around her and daring her to do anything but finish this perilous dance.

Amelia's close enough now that when she sighs it's as good as a kiss. Their mouths are open, their lips wet, and their breath shared. Just the finest of lines between them.

It's when Amelia finally speaks—finally moves her lips— that it's all over. Just the barest of touches as her lips try to form that first letter. She cannot finish saying Laura's name without their lips brushing together.

It's done. Laura holds onto the table with one hand and grasps Amelia's hip with the other as she dives down and consumes Amelia. All fire. Wet and hot fire that burns her belly and reaches out to fingers and toes.

They breathe in abortive messy gasps, punctuated by lips and tongues and the graze of teeth.

It's exquisite and right and could go on forever, but there are footsteps on the stairs. She forces herself away until her back presses against the wall and she presses her hand to her mouth. Amelia looks at her with hunger, as if she's trying not to pant.

"Laura?"

She closes her eyes at the sound of her husband's voice.

When she opens them again, she finds Amelia stricken. She knows that nothing she can do can get them out of the mess she's dragged them into.

"Coming down," she says instead. Her voice as piqued as the rest of her.

"Have you seen Miss Wright up there," he whispers loudly.

Amelia takes one moment that's truthfully infinitesimal but feels far more substantial. Then Amelia isn't flushed or breathless. Her thumb and finger swipe over her mouth and remove any smudges. "I'm here," she says. "Was looking for Laura and the nickel tour."

Michel frowns at her, but only for a moment. Before he was a foppish diplomat, he spent years operating in the French Resistance. He's no fool, and he's good at masking things. He steps back and waves down the stairs. "I think your date is getting ready to leave. Something about wanting to see more of you before you leave tomorrow."

He says it politely enough, but there's something nasty there under the surface. Laura feels primeval in her anger, and whether it's directed toward her husband or Chalmers, she can't be sure.

Amelia doesn't look at her as they descend the stairs. Laura's back is ramrod straight, and she's as rigid as a board, coiled tight with all kinds of emotions that Michel's brother would have been ashamed of and would turn away Amelia if she could see them.

Halfway down, cool knuckles brush against her wrist.

It could be the mere swing of Amelia's arms that form the contact, but Laura grasps the touch like a lifeline and uses it to pull herself out of a mire of her own making.

Chalmers is chatty and handsy when they reach the bottom of the stairs. His lips are cold and wet against Laura's cheek, and his hands large and clumsy in hers.

He stands so close that he inspires an uncommon wrath in Laura.

He helps Amelia with her stole and ignores her while she puts on her gloves. She drops her handbag in the juggle and Laura is the first to the scene. She stoops down to pick it up, and their hands touch as she returns it. Amelia's fingertips press into the space between her knuckles.

"We should get together sometime," she says. Her voice is high and loud, but to Laura it seems a whisper, as if they're the only ones there.

"I'd love to," she replies. "We could catch up."

"Soon." From Amelia, the word's a promise. Enough of one that Laura barely seethes when Chalmers wraps his arm around Amelia's waist and speaks with his lips too close to her ear.

At the car, Amelia turns, takes a breath deep into her chest, and smiles.

And for the night.

And the days to come.

That's enough.

CHAPTER 18

AMELIA DOES NOT RETURN TO New York immediately. The local press is breathless when they note she's taken a role as another of those "women who served and then gave it all up after the war" pictures and has decided to stay on in DC "for research."

"I'll actually be meeting with one such woman," she says.

Laura's cheek twitches when she reads that in the paper. Michel asks if she's all right, and she tells him just how fine she is.

She doesn't know where Amelia's staying in the city, and she is sorely tempted, twice, to use the resources at her disposal to find out, but the last time she tried that—when attempting a background check on the nanny—it resulted in a... very embarrassing dressing down in front of her coworkers.

But she's tempted to risk it anyway.

Except... except Amelia has her address. She knows where Laura lives. She can stop by whenever she likes to say hello, and she really ought to because Laura can't be the one doing the chasing all the time. She's got a whole world to protect, damn it.

When she arrives home one day, there are flowers sitting on the kitchen counter. She smirks. They're simpler than the last set, but they're all red, white, and blue, and she feels that silly pang she always does when it comes to patriotism.

There's a note tucked into them. "Got any tips for the newest spy on the French front?"

It's signed with a hotel name and room number.

She slips the card into her pocket for safekeeping and puts the flowers on the table. When Michel sees them later, he frowns but doesn't say anything.

Laura doesn't make it to the hotel. Instead, the next morning, she stands in her office, watching the news and crushing the card in her hand because Amelia's there on the television again. She ducks down, and the flash of camera lights reflects off her big glasses and glossy hair. The newscaster talks about how she's being forced into an emergency hearing concerning communists in Hollywood.

Her whole department cowers that day as she stalks the halls and lurks over too clever agents and analysts. No one can tell her why Amelia Wright is being brought before the House Un-American Activities Committee.

"But chatter's through the roof because of it," one newer analyst finally confesses. "If she isn't already working for the Soviets, they'll be trying to recruit her by the afternoon."

"She isn't." Laura's sure of that.

That afternoon she travels to the Hill to sit in on the hearing. She sits demurely, legs crossed at the ankle, and ignores the few faces around that recognize her. Most don't.

Up front, Amelia's back is ramrod straight as she answers some questions and refuses to answer even more. The committee is tired and angry, none more so than Chalmers, who growls his way through the proceedings and glares hard at the top of Amelia's head every time she looks down at her hands.

Finally, a break is called, and Amelia stands and asks one of her escorts a question. She's stiff as she makes her way out into the hallway and through the reporters.

Laura's much more nimble, and sifts through the crowd as if it were sand. She follows Amelia and her escort to a small meeting room. One she isn't going to get into without throwing around a lot of names.

The room next door is open though, and after tucking her heels into her waistband and throwing the strap of her purse across her whole body, she climbs out the only window, closing it with slippery fingertips.

She inches along carefully and is grateful the room is on the side of the building and she's half hidden in the shade. Otherwise, she'd be the one splayed across the newspapers later as everyone wonders who the hell is crawling along the outside of Capitol Hill.

Her big toe slips, and she has to grip the crevices between the stones a little tighter. She's rather proud when the string of curses that escape her lips is short.

And she's lucky that the only one to hear the expletives is Amelia, who pops open the window and leans out looking startled, wary, and so very, very tired. Seeing who it is, she sighs.

"You couldn't knock?"

"I didn't want to be forward."

Amelia shakes her head and offers a hand that Laura gratefully takes. "I would have been happy to see you versus the rest of those vultures."

They don't let go even after Amelia pulls her in. She stands too close and the wind whips into the room, ruining both their fastidious curls. "I just thought it might look odd, being who we both are."

Amelia tilts her head even as the pads of her fingers stroke Laura's hand. "Who are we?" she asks, her voice a thrilling whisper.

Laura wants to swallow. Somehow, around Amelia she finds herself turned into one of those All-American aw shucks kind of boys.

Instead Laura comes just an inch closer and revels in the delicious sensation of standing so near. There's something intoxicating and heady about the way they flirt, all up close and dancing on that razor's edge. It makes it all feel dangerous.

And definitely not boring.

"An Oscar-winning actress." She's staring at Amelia's lips. The color she's wearing is demure—her one nod to the forum she's appearing in. "And a—"

Amelia leans up, and Laura braces herself for what's sure to be a wonderful kiss.

"Spy?" It's a question instead. Right before Amelia steps back explosively, flinging Laura's hand away and stalking toward a small platter of muffins and scones on the table.

Laura's hands fall uselessly to her side.

"You couldn't waltz in the front because then they'd all think little Miss Super Spy was a big flaming Communist."

"That's not true..." It is, in fact, a little true.

Amelia snatches up a muffin and throws it at her.

"Did you just throw—"

She throws another one too.

"Are you quite finished," she begs as she bats a scone away from her head.

"Some big knight in shining armor you are, Laura Wright! Skulking in the back and asking me to do the same. Can't even go vouch for me."

"And how should I do that, hmm? Oh Amelia's marvelous. She made me come more times in one night than my husband has in our whole marriage. Won't you please let her go?"

"I'm not asking you to out me! Jesus Christ. But, you know, telling 'em you know me, and that I'm not sitting in bed making moon eyes at Stalin might be a little bit of a start."

Laura's quiet a moment. "That's an elaborate image."

Amelia has her arms crossed, and her body nominally turned away from Laura. "So's the one of you and your husband." She looks Laura up and down with no small amount of pity.

"It was a joke."

"Sure."

"He's brilliant in bed." He is certainly not terrible.

Amelia sniffs. "I've no doubt."

"You're being—"

"What," Amelia asks, eyebrow raised.

Laura looks down at her shoes, still stuffed into her skirt waist. Between that, the flying pastries, and Amelia's nonplussed expression, she feels very foolish.

Amelia sighs. "How about this... when you want to help me and not just try to take advantage by consoling—"

"I am doing no such thing!"

"—me. Then we can talk."

"I didn't just come here to console." She sounds a little petulant, but she'd never admit it.

Amelia crosses her arms. Actually crosses them. As if Laura is some shirty customer at the old diner.

"I can help."

"Are you going to go tell 'em I'm not a commie?"

"No."

"Then there's the door, Agent."

Why is it people only ever use that title when they are irritated with Laura? It is never a sign of respect, but more like the "Miss Wright" uttered by bothered school marms in her youth.

"I could talk to Chalmers. Perhaps he can smooth things over."

Amelia huffs. "He's already trying. Pretty sure he thinks I'll take him with me if I fold."

Laura blinks. "He's a communist?"

"No, but he's so light in the loafers he practically floats."

"So's half the Hill."

Amelia rolls her eyes as if this isn't brand new information.

Laura ventures, "Do you often date men who?..."

"If I don't want to worry about them getting ideas, yeah."

Laura pulls her shoes out of her waistband and drops them on the floor and then leans against the table.

Oh.

Oh.

She's ashamed at how long it took her to work out exactly what Amelia's been doing with the line of men she's been dating. It's the sort of sluggish mental acuity she'd expect from Michel or her old OSS colleagues.

Amelia doesn't tell her to leave again, but she does sit down at the table, pokes a scone with her finger and studiously ignores Laura. When they call for her to return to the hearing, Laura comes over and squeezes her forearm, tells her it will be okay, and then hides behind the door like a big fat coward.

She doesn't—she can't—suffer through the rest of the hearing, so she makes her way back to work and tries to understand how Amelia came under fire to begin with. Particularly if she's a lynchpin in some sort of homosexual consortium. That's the sort of thing that would normally keep a person far from this kind of suspicion.

Which means someone is setting her up.

She thinks about calling Amelia from her untraceable office line that night. Amelia's life has become a mystery, and Laura feels, for a variety of reasons, that she needs to solve it. But even if her call can't be traced, she has to assume Amelia's under surveillance.

At home, before dinner, she idly flips through a magazine and bounces her leg nervously. When he comes home later than usual, Michel is unshaven and oddly quiet.

It gnaws on her, the question of who is setting Amelia up. There are the usual suspects, chiefly the Russians. Yet the why of it, doesn't make sense.

She keeps circling around and around the problem until, somehow, she finds herself sneaking into Amelia's hotel at half past eleven that night. It's not the hardest mission she's ever had, but it does require two costume changes, a wig, and a Swiss accent that she has on good authority is terrible.

Sneaking into Amelia's room itself is the most difficult part. There's a man that screams "agent" standing at the end of the hall and his gaze forces her to duck her head and keep walking. And walking.

And walking.

And ultimately slipping out a window and crawling around to Amelia's room.

She thanks God for small favors when she finds the room empty. Having Amelia catch her climbing in through the window for the second time in a day would be... embarrassing.

She's settling down to inspect Amelia's room for surveillance when a key in the lock tells her she has company. Lurking in the shadows, she sighs when she sees it's just Amelia, all alone.

Much of that Hollywood sheen has wasted away over the course of the day. Strands of hair have come loose from the previously immaculate do, and there are no glasses to hide the dark bags forming under her eyes. Amelia sighs and leans back against the door. The motion exposes a long expanse of neck that's pale under all the powder she now wears.

For a moment, even with the fatigue wearing her down, Amelia is some kind of portrait. All done in oils and illuminated only by the faint yellow glow of a lamp.

As if she's aware of Laura's mute scrutiny, Amelia tenses.

Her fingers curl around her bag as she straightens up.

She flips the light switch and immediately relaxes when she sees who it is waiting for her. "Thank God. I thought— well I don't know what I thought, but I'm sure glad it's you." She even smiles.

Laura flips a switch on a device in her purse and steps closer. The lights in the room flicker. "Not an assassin?"

"Or an overly enthusiastic fan, or whatever. How'd you get in? Because there's a guy in the hall, pretending he's not watching me and about a half dozen more down in the lobby—"

"Amelia, I'd love to discuss the details, but I'm afraid we don't have time. I've just flipped a switch that will ruin any surveillance taking place in this room."

Amelia's brow furrows with confusion, her bright eyes wide. "So... shouldn't we have all the time?"

"Yes. If you aren't being watched, absolutely. If you are..." She looks to the door, waiting for the shadow to blot out the light and tell her someone's there. "Well, they'll be coming to call. Won't they?"

"I don't get it. I mean, this stupid hearing aside, why would someone be watching me? I'm not actually a spy."

"I think... it's what you said today about Chalmers."

Amelia blanches.

"You know things, Amelia. You have secrets that could unmake half this country if you chose to share them—"

"Except these aren't the kind of secrets a girl goes and shares, Laura. I'd be taking myself down too."

"Before the hearing, yes. But now you're being tagged a communist. You've got nothing to lose."

"I've got plenty!" Her hand strikes her chest when she says it. She's so sure. So positive. Desperate.

Laura has to reach out and put her hands on Amelia's arms. It's not the same as the hug she feels she should give her, but the contact soothes her and seems to calm Amelia.

"I know you do," she says softly, "but the rest of the world doesn't."

This close it's easy to be familiar, to feel that wanting that thrums through every bit of her. Amelia's just a little shorter than her, so when she looks up, the light catches in her eyes and brings out an amber hue that makes her gaze warm.

She licks her lips.

Those warm eyes settle on her mouth. Then Amelia swallows and looks back up at her.

She speaks before Amelia can say something wonderful. "I need you to make a list."

She quirks one eyebrow. Amelia's confused. "A list?"

"Someone reported you and set all this in motion. We have to find that person. Ex-boyfriends. Colleagues who hate you. Lovers. Former... family connections. All of them."

She tries to ignore the flinch when she says "lovers." Tries not to think about what it could mean. Tries not to think about the last few years, how far they've come, and how much they couldn't have.

"Okay," Amelia says evenly. She takes a step closer. She can be so still, so smooth. She has a poker face Laura's agents would be envious of. "So we make a list."

Laura's hands are still on Amelia's arms, and she thinks it wouldn't be too difficult to pull her toward her and kiss her senseless. It wouldn't be difficult or wrong, but perhaps ill-timed.

She pulls. Amelia comes willingly. She tips her face upward, and her eyes start to fall closed, and Laura's eyes start to close too. Just so she can enjoy the sensation, so she can have something tactile and memorable.

And then there's three knocks at the door. Steady and sure.

They freeze. So close. She can see the eyelash that's fallen on Amelia's cheek and smell the powder she's recently applied to her nose.

"You should get that," she whispers into her hair.

Amelia swallows.

"Miss Wright, this is maintenance. We're afraid there may be a leak in your room."

Amelia's breathing quickly, and while Laura would like to think it's due to her proximity, she knows it has everything to do with the man at the door.

"You'll be all right," she tells her.

Then she does kiss her, but it's quick and meant to comfort, and it's far, far too easy. A kiss dropped onto Amelia's perfectly painted lips. She never used to wear such purposeful shades.

Another kiss at her hairline.

"Just act naturally."

Amelia pushes away, smooths down the front of her dress, and walks toward the door with her head held high.

And Laura escapes back out the window.

It's Friday. Amelia's second appearance before the thugs and brutes of HUAC. Hard-looking men with smiles sharp as knives and hands graceful as wrecking balls.

They, Chalmers and his "colleagues," demand Amelia tell them what she knows. Tell them who she knows. Laura watches from her office. Periodically, they all take breaks from their work to watch the proceedings and make crude jokes.

In the hearing, Amelia appears cool. Collected.

The questions, accusations, and constant needling seem to flow right off the persona she honed and hardened out west.

But then they mention her family, and back in her office, Laura sighs. Amelia is very particular when it comes to her family.

It isn't the snide remarks about her uncle or the insinuations about her one-legged brother. Those make her back rigid as a board.

It's her father. They mention the one dead Maldonado, and Amelia's hands go to her lap.

He apparently went to a meeting once.

Amelia leans in.

Details are lost on a TV screen. Everything's a little fuzzy and nuances that jump out at you in person disappear.

But Laura can still see Amelia's growing anger over the maligning of her father. Finally she snaps. "I think that's enough, don't you?"

The head of the committee has been sitting up there, prying into the lives of American citizens for half a decade, and he is not a man accustomed to being silenced. "I don't think it is," he counters, like a school teacher chiding a student.

"What you want is a list of names, isn't it, Congressman?"

It is. It absolutely is.

The room is quiet. The one on screen, and the one Laura stands in.

Amelia leans into the microphone, cool and calm. She's a statue carved from marble and set before Congress. "Just give me a few days to prepare it." She glances around her. Her gaze falls on Chalmers, who suddenly sits back in his chair and looks piqued. "I'll give you an *extraordinary* list."

If she'd left it there, it might have been nothing. Just another Hollywood harlot brought to heel by the big bad boys of DC and forced to bare it all.

But Amelia...Amelia has never met a script she couldn't devour or a scene she couldn't explode. So Amelia makes an exit. Waltzes out of the room with bravado to spare, and nothing in the way of an official dismissal.

There's shouting, and someone pounds a gavel. Lights flash, and Amelia—God damn it—Amelia *grins*.

The furor's so loud they probably hear it in the White House.

CHAPTER 19

LAURA'S ATTEMPT AT TRIAGE DOESN'T start with a visit to Amelia or a conversation with her superiors. It starts with a visit to a smoky jazz lounge. The kind that's all dark leather, darker walls, and the only real light comes from the stage where a woman's wrapped around a microphone, singing old standards in a sultry timbre.

The cigarette smoke forms a haze that Laura moves through discretely. The lounge isn't crowded, but it isn't empty either. All the patrons are focused on the stage, and the waitresses keep their own gazes averted as they move between the tables.

It's a good place for a meeting. Out in Baltimore, just far enough away from DC that Laura won't see people she knows. Not unless, of course, they're engaged in equally nasty business… or following her.

The woman she's seeing is decked out in a deep magenta dress that complements her copper-colored hair. She's smoking a cigarette as she watches the performance, and her only acknowledgment of Laura is the way she slides over in the booth to allow Laura to sit.

Laura orders a drink using a polite accent that's tinged with bits of Baltimore, making sure she removes any of the polish her usual tone carries. And she watches the singer too.

"We don't do this often enough." The other woman sighs. She's playful. Always playful. The cat and the mouse again.

"Thanks for taking the time."

The woman smiles. "Anything for you, my dear Laura." She takes Laura's glass from the waitress and sets it down. The shiny scars on her forearm are caught in the dim light, but the waitress says nothing. "Now, what is this about?"

She watches Laura with those watery blue eyes of hers. She knows why Laura is sitting in this lounge, pretending to enjoy her drink. Judith Bashkirov—once and future Judy Bass (or Hayseed if you're Amelia)—is a clever woman.

But she likes her games, likes to toy with her prey. And her friends.

So, Laura doesn't answer her.

"I was shocked to see all the news about our little friend from 3C." She's playing a complimentary tune on the lip of her glass. "I never would have guessed her for a sympathizer."

It could be conversation. But Laura thinks it isn't.

"And now with that list? Gotta love her flair for the dramatic." Judith rests her chin on her hand and keeps watching the stage. Her American accent is so aw shucks. So perfectly Midwest. So much better than Laura's own snobbish accent, drilled into her by schools in America and England. "She always had a crush on you, you know, back at the Sebastian."

"Did she? I never would have guessed."

"Most people wouldn't, but I was half convinced you were recruiting her to your network." So pleased with herself. "So I paid attention."

"Yes, I remember finding you skulking about in rooms that weren't your own. Right before you set fire to the building."

"We were both there when it went up in flames." She always looks a little mad talking about the past, especially the violent bits.

"But I didn't start the fire."

She shrugs, no desire to deny the truth.

"I need to know what your plans for her are."

"Mine?" Judith's coyly shocked.

Laura stares.

This time Judith smirks. "I don't work for them anymore. Remember? You burned me half to death, and they left me in the cold?"

She came to Laura a year later, haggard and desperate for a handout. One Laura reluctantly gave. Spies are dangerous, but a good spy with a debt is useful.

"You have connections."

Talking with Judith is always like a dance. One wrong step and you're on her toes, and then she's furious. Much like she is now, suddenly. Eyes wide and hard smile replaced by pursed lips and a tight jaw.

"Awfully fond of 3C aren't you?"

"Fond of all the girls we knew back then."

"Oh, I seriously doubt that."

"I'm fond of you, aren't I?" She rewards Judith with a brittle smile that the other woman basks in.

If others knew the games she and Judith play, they'd call her cunning. And too cruel. Sometimes when she plays them, she sees the ghosts of those she's loved, standing just out of focus and looking so terribly disappointed in her.

Judith watches her and scoots closer. "How fond," she asks, boldly flirtatious.

"I've shown you before."

So terribly disappointed.

"Show me again." Her knee bumps against Laura's, and it's no accident. Judith has been trained for years to be in complete control of her body, even when she's looking at Laura as if she's a morsel to be devoured.

Laura puts her hand on Judith's knee and pushes it away. "Someone's set her up. I just need to know who."

She laughs, throaty and rich and cold. "I think, Laura, that 3C wasn't the only one with a crush back then."

"She's a stranger in our world. I just want to make sure she stays that way."

"And if I'd known about these feelings back then, I would have slit her throat." She leans in close enough that Laura can feel the ghost of her breath on her skin. "Ear to ear."

She turns so that she and Judith are near nose to nose. She can see the freckles concealed by powder. "Well, then, it's a good thing I've always been better than you at concealing my crushes."

Judith licks her lips. She's hungry and angry, and that's always when she's her most dangerous. Sometimes that makes her exquisite, an awful diversion from so much of Laura's day to day.

But right now, Judith is a distraction.

"I'm in the cold, Laura. And soon your crush," she spits the word out with a contempt it seems only Russians can muster, "will be too. And this winter? Oh for that woman, it's gonna be brutal."

She puts her own people on guard for Amelia. Kids she trained herself that have no affiliation with the CIA, kids who might not even know it exists. Too many of the grunts that fill out the ranks of the agency are former police and military. Big guys in dark suits who scream "up to no good" as they crowd into cars and fill up seats in hotel lobbies.

They're a threatening group of men, to be sure, but they're hardly capable of quietly trailing someone.

Laura's network is.

She sends a squeaky clean college boy in a sweater and tie. It's nasty business, but the news says Amelia looks... strong.

Laura can't bear the idea of checking for herself. She doesn't have the time if she wants to save her. She needs to work.

She takes her business to the congressman from California, Clyde Doyle. The man's got a hawkish nose that threatens to dip into his bourbon with each slurping sip, and he sniffs each bite of fish before slipping it into his mouth.

Laura crosses her legs, smiles, and talks to him about Michel, their children, the projects in his district, and wines his wife might like. They talk about everything but the woman on trial.

Until dessert comes. He digs in, and Laura rests her elbows on the table, lights a cigarette, and says, "Nasty business with that starlet."

He grunts an agreement and assures her that Amelia Wright will give up all her comrades.

"I just wonder who gave her up." Laura keeps her voice breathy and lets herself sound confused. "She's always seemed so above all... that."

It earns her a patronizing smile and a light pat on the hand.

She presses for more information, but the congressman knows nothing. Just insists it was anonymous. Only the Chairman knows who gave him the tip.

The Chairman is Mr. John Woods, and Mr. John Woods hates Laura. He doesn't like her old money, her Mid-Atlantic accent, or the fact that she's a woman.

But he likes her husband all right, because Michel is a very likable man.

Likable until Laura stands across from Michel in the kitchen and says, "I need your help."

He's popping the top off a beer and has his shirt sleeves rolled up. It's always been one of his most endearing looks. The dark hair running from hand to elbow and the bony narrow wrists.

The lid lands in the sink with a clink, and he raises an eyebrow. "What do you want me to do?"

"An old friend needs help. I was hoping you might speak to Congressman Woods on their behalf."

He sips his beer, and the noise is cacophonous this late at night, with the children in bed and all the radios and televisions turned off.

He pulls the bottle away with a smack. "A friend."

"She was here at the party—"

He sets the beer down on the counter and crosses his arms. He knows who Laura means. He has to. Michel is not a stupid man. But he stares at her expectantly, waiting for her to say the name.

"She's innocent," she says instead. "Someone's setting her up, and I've a mind to find out who."

"Why?"

"Because she's an old friend—"

He shakes his head, and it's been a long few days. The pomade that keeps his coif in place is starting to fail. A dark lock of hair falls into his eyes. "Why do you think someone's setting her up?"

"Because Amelia's not a spy."

"That you know of."

"No," she says evenly. "Period."

Michel's jaw sets, and he glares at the tile floor just in front of Laura's feet. Blindly, he reaches for his beer and takes another gulp. "She's offered a list—"

"Under duress and definitely not the kind they're expecting."

He pulls the bottle from his lips with a pop. "The other night, she was in our home."

"Invited by Congressman Chalmers—"

He's bitter. Absolutely bitter. "Walking the halls as if she owned the place. Skulking—"

Oh no.

"Michel."

What did he do?

He finishes his beer off in one long draught. "If she wasn't in our home to spy, then what was she here for?"

Me.

Laura wants to tell him Amelia was in their home for her. That she'd come because Laura had pestered her until she'd said yes. That she'd invited herself up the stairs and into their sanctum because she'd needed to see Laura. Speak to Laura. Touch Laura.

But saying all that isn't so easy. They're not words that can fall carelessly from the lips.

Because she knows what will surely chase right after them.

She hugs herself with one arm and looks away, toward the window. There's no moon tonight, just a glassy darkness that looks so terrifying and remote from the comfort of a warm kitchen.

Michel sighs, and his footfalls sound on the kitchen tiles as he paces. When he throws his bottle at the sink. it shatters, and she shudders.

Laura flinches and is briefly grateful the children are upstairs and far away.

"For you." Disgust laces Michel's his voice.

"You're the one who turned her in," Laura counters.

He laughs, and it's as bitter as borax. "I thought she was a spy, but she was just here to seduce my wife."

Laura laughs too. Not as bitterly. She's never carried the same illusions as Michel when it comes to their marriage. It's always been a tenuous treaty to serve their own interests. Not—not whatever he's currently grieving.

"You've got it all wrong, dear. I was the one who pursued her."

He looks up sharply. "That's supposed to make me feel better?"

"No. But I'm a woman of facts, Michel, and I'd like to keep it that way." She tilts her head, lifting her chin. "What precisely did you tell Woods about her?"

He's surly and chastened, and Laura's steeling herself for as brutal an interrogation as she's ever given when the phone rings.

It's loud and obnoxious, and never a good sound after ten at night.

Michel glares at her.

A challenge.

Because they both know the phone never rings for him so late. It's always for her, only for her.

It keeps going. The shrill ring measures out the long moments as the two of them stare at one another.

The conversation will be over Michel says with a look.

But this is just as important.

He turns his back on her. *It always is* he seems to say.

He fetches another beer, and she picks up the phone and answers with a terse, "Yes."

It's one of the kids she has following Amelia. "She's gone on a trip," the boy says. "We've stopped at a diner an hour out of town."

Shit.

Laura breathes in long and slow. A meditative kind of breath, not unlike the ones she took when the contractions started and the twins came along.

There's a crack and hiss behind her as Michel opens another beer. He's watching her.

Waiting.

Wary.

And Amelia's running.

"Keep her there," she says in a low voice. "I'm on my way."

"Urgent business?" Michel asks, lips half wrapped around the mouth of his beer.

She tsks as she looks distractedly around the room for where she last left her purse. "State secrets, dear."

"Just be careful," he says, and he's frustrated. The way he gets when she keeps secrets he desperately wants to learn.

"Aren't I always?"

"No. You're not." His chin juts out, as if he's saying something profound and dangerous. "Especially when it comes to women."

She spies her purse, there on the counter behind Michel. "That makes two of us." She comes close, and he doesn't bother to move so she reaches past him. "When your girlfriend stops, do make sure she doesn't sleep in my bed? I've just changed the sheets."

They never talk about his dalliances. Just as they normally never talk about hers. It's peeling off bandages they are both normally perfectly happy to keep intact.

He calls out after her. "You know, at least the company I keep is loyal to this country."

So is the company Laura keeps.

Even Judith, that spy stuck out in the cold, maintains allegiances to Laura, who is loyal to America.

She refuses to engage him, not interested in having a fight neither of them can afford or picking at the scabs festering in this "marriage."

She kisses his cheek, squeezes his arm, and walks away.

"Goodnight, Michel."

CHAPTER 20

HER BROTHER AND THE OTHER boys always said—say—
she has a temper. *So short she's practically Irish.*

And at home, Amelia does have a temper. She's
wedged her foot up her family's backsides so many times she
confuses the idiots for shoes.

But on the job, she's demure. She giggles, acts sly, and
never raises her voice because Amelia Wright is the portrait
of perfection, the perfect lady who keeps her cool.

Threatening to list all the queers between Hollywood
and DC is not what a perfect lady would do.

In the heat of it, under the lights and in the crowded
hall, it feels really, really good to promise a list and flounce
out. She walks to her hired car and feels like Jesse Owens
must have when he won that first Gold.

Then the agent escorting her, shuts the door, and all
the flash and pomp of the trial is a dull roar. That's when
Amelia realizes she's done about the stupidest thing she
could have done, short of being seen going down on a lady
in the Kremlin.

So, she sneaks out of her hotel room, and she goes for a
drive.

A real long drive.

The hardest part is dodging the suits who follow her as soon as her Jaguar is on the road. Part of the whole appeal of a real long drive is not having guys sitting right behind her on the road with the glare of their headlights filling her car.

Losing them involves a few twists and turns, and she runs a few red lights. But after they're lost in her rearview, she heads north, toward home. She's got a place in Long Island and an apartment in the city, and either of those is better than pacing that gilded cage she's staying at in DC.

An hour into her drive, she gets hungry for something more than the fear that's been filling her belly, and she pulls off into an all-night diner that promises her greasy sandwiches and stout coffee.

The flow of coffee's constant, but the sandwich takes a while. The waitress comes over three times, blushing profusely and apologizing.

"We're just really backed up," she says. Amelia'd be inclined to believe it if there were more people in the diner. But there's just a family, a couple of teens at the counter, and a trucker.

The teens look over their shoulders to stare at her as if they know her, and she ducks her head, pours more cream into her coffee, and ponders skipping the sandwich.

Then, the kids pay and head out, and Amelia watches them for something to do. One of them goes to his car, while the other crosses the gravel lot to lean into the window of a car that's only just come in.

Words are exchanged.

Cash too.

The kid straightens up, looks through the window of the diner straight at Amelia. She glances down at her coffee.

She's got her hands wrapped around the cup so tight the ceramic's like to crack.

When she glances back up, the kid is gone and Laura God damned Wright is coming through the door of the diner. The bell rings overhead.

She's dressed in something she must have worn to the office. Amelia herself operates in two modes—glamorous movie star and lady about to go weeding in the yard. But Laura…Laura's just got the one mode. Sophisticated. Smart tailored dresses and perfect cashmere coats that don't make her look like a sack.

It'd rankle Amelia if she wasn't so damned head over heels for her.

When she's close enough, Amelia hisses. "Did you really have two bobbysoxers spying on me?"

Laura chuckles. "More than two, actually. Any particular reason they had to follow you to Maryland?"

"I was bored."

Laura brushes her coat aside to put one hand on her hip. She purses her lips.

Miraculously, Amelia's sandwich arrives around the same time, and she opts to focus on it rather than the judgmental spy looming over her.

"Are you gonna sit," she asks around a mouthful of patty melt, "or just keep standing there like a statue?"

"You're being tried for treason—"

"Only haphazardly—"

"And stalked by federal agents—"

"Who I managed to lose—"

"And your first thought was, 'Jolly holiday in Maryland'?"

The patty melt is definitely a two-hander, but Amelia switches to one hand so she can reach for her coffee and take another swig. In this particular moment she is playing the character of "flippant wunderkind" because if she doesn't play that character, she's pretty sure she's gonna throw up all over the tabletop.

Jesus what was she thinking? She *is* being tried for treason. She promised a list that could get her killed. She is being stalked by federal agents—and bobbysoxers—and her sort of ex. A casual drive up to New York is not the wisest idea.

The flippant thing must work, because when she doesn't respond, Laura huffs and collapses onto the bench across from her. "You can't run," she says, equal measures of urgency and sincerity. She looks at Amelia with those earnest dark eyes of hers. The same sort of look she gave her when she showed up in the Radio City Music Hall bathroom and professed her undying love.

Amelia swallows and sets the rest of the sandwich on the plate carefully. "I know."

"So why all this?"

"I spend my whole life in front of cameras and microphones. Not really keen on it when I'm taking a dump."

Laura wrinkles her nose. "Spectacular image there."

"You asked."

"Was it really the surveillance?"

"How screwed up is your life that you think I need more than that as a reason?"

Laura reaches across the table to snag Amelia's coffee and take a sip. "Pretty exceptional currently. My husband gave me an ultimatum tonight." It's conversational. Laura's always got a knack for taking the most terrifying of circumstances and churning out something... informal.

"How caveman," Amelia says, "He threaten to cut off your allowance if you didn't start shaping up?"

"No. He intimated, with stern looks, that he'd leave me if I chased after you."

The look Laura gives her is enough to tell her how hung up on that marriage Laura isn't. It also sets a furnace right in the center of Amelia, boiling away the last of her fear and replacing it with something much more pleasant.

"So, here you are," Amelia says, surprised at how even her voice sounds. She crosses her ankles.

Laura's just as even. She's one of those steady gals. "Here I am."

Amelia swallows. Looks down at her plate and offers the first piece of food she sees. "Pickle?"

They walk out of the diner together. Laura's half a head taller than Amelia and keeps looking over at her as she scans the parking lot. She's standing close too, and Amelia half expects her to put an arm around her waist as she escorts her to her car.

Amelia wouldn't protest.

"You," Amelia clears her throat, "you need a ride?"

Laura looks at her as if she's a very pleasant little idiot. "No. I'll follow in my car. In case any of the agents from the hotel catch up to us."

"We're an hour away."

"Yes, and you're driving a sports car of which there are, what? Twelve in the world?" Laura motions to Amelia's

Jaguar XK120. It's ostentatious, a little manly, and it's hers. She's tweaked bits and pieces of it herself and has promised Clark Gable a race next time he gets his older one in town.

She grouses. "There's more 'an twelve."

"Not on this seaboard." Suddenly Laura turns and puts both her hands on Amelia's shoulders. It forces Amelia to look up at her, right in the eye, forces her to see how calm and confident Laura is, like a soldier out of her last picture. "I'll be right behind you," she says. "Nothing to it."

"You're making me a little nervous, Laura. Like they might do something to me if they catch me."

She steps closer. Pushes Amelia back toward her car and into the darkness that surrounds it. Their thighs brush. Amelia's insides leap, and she can just see the kiss Laura's about to plant on her lips. So, she looks up at her eyes wide, lips parted.

"Not as long as I'm here," she says, and she leans in to kiss Amelia but stops when another car pulls into the lot and an old man hobbles out.

As soon as she's gone, Amelia feels colder, and she buttons up her coat and pops the collar before climbing into her car.

They drive.

Laura hangs back far enough that Amelia loses her on some of the bends. The idea is to, at minimum, make it to Pennsylvania before Amelia needs to sleep. She's had enough coffee, and she's hopped up on enough fear that it isn't too outrageous an idea.

Until she sees the headlights winking in her rearview. The other car is coming up fast—and it's not the Cadillac Laura was driving. She's just got a hint of its shape and those headlights to go on, but she thinks it's a Chevy.

Like one of the ones she lost back in DC.

They slow down to match her speed when they're close enough. She gives her car some gas. The Chevy matches.

She slows down.

The Chevy doesn't pass her.

Laura's headlights aren't in sight—there could be a lot of reasons for that—but Amelia's not gonna drive like normal and hope Laura's just a little farther behind.

She hooks it down a farm road.

The Chevy follows.

Then their car leaps forward with a roar and slams into her backend.

Amelia's a good driver.

She's been chased down by more cars that most can count, and she always, always, gets away.

But this time it's late, she's exhausted, and she's being chased down by a car apparently rebuilt like a goddamned tank.

The odds that she used to be so good at tweaking to her favor are decidedly against her. So, when he catches up with her on another curve and smashes the front end of his tank into the back end of her zippy Jaguar, she goes into a skid she never planned for in this car.

Doesn't matter how wide her tires are when they lock up and lose traction. The whole car slides off the road and down into the slippery grass—wet from that midnight dew.

It doesn't flip. Thank God. A sports car like this has a low center of gravity and she manages to direct it just enough during the slide that the front end catches and crunches against a boulder instead of the side that would have flipped them.

But it hurts. The whole world rattles and scratches at her and then clangs to a stop that sends her heart, stomach, and the rest of her insides right into her mouth.

She's gotta go. She's gotta get away. She tries to turn the car's engine over, but it's *tick tick ticking* and hissing like the radiator and engine block are both cracked.

She beats the steering wheel.

Stops.

Getting mad's not gonna keep her alive.

There's the creak of the other car coming to a stop, followed by doors opening and gravel crunching under expensive shoes.

Her headlights are smashed but theirs aren't. They're illuminating a field on the other side of the boulder. Freshly planted with big ol' corridors of dirt that she knows will be a horror show to run through in her heels.

There's something wet in her eyes—right below where her headache's developing. She wipes it away. Doesn't look at her hand because she doesn't need to see the blood that's likely darkening it.

She couldn't have worn loafers tonight? Loafers would have made sense. And been comfortable. And—

A weapon. She needs something to fight these guys with.

Or a friend. A friend might be nice. Laura driving up like the cavalry and talking these fellas out of whatever murderous plans they're harboring.

But beyond that one car there's just the night.

Goddamn it, Laura.

"Put the gun away," one of the men says. "No shooting her."

"But she's still alive."

"But it's got to look like an accident, you idiot. Bullet holes aren't an accident."

"So what—we beat her to death?"

Okay. Okay. Jesus.

Okay Amelia's got a lump forming on her forehead and everything's a little foggy, but the two goons who ran her off the road are definitely planning to kill her. Kill her real dead.

And it's just Amelia.

Maybe about to die.

She carefully—quietly—undoes the seatbelt latch and reaches for the door. If there's no plan to use guns, then they'll have to chase her down.

She swallows because wow is everything wobbly.

She can run for it.

The whole car shakes as one of the goons falls into it.

Then there's grunting and groaning and the sound of a fist hitting a sack of meat.

Amelia turns around in her seat and watches as Laura Wright beats the ever loving shit out of two men twice her size.

All while in heels.

As fights go—Amelia hasn't seen many outside of a ring—it's vicious and quick. Laura's all efficient with eyes alight like murder.

Watching her repeatedly bash a man's head into the side of a car, she can just catch a glimpse of the resistance leader and spy that made the war a living hell.

She stops her savage beating when Amelia finally climbs out of the car. The two of them stare at each other. Laura's hand is wrapped around an unconscious man's collar and her knuckles are all bruised, and Amelia just stands there, clutching her bag and working like hell to keep herself upright.

Because things. Things are real wrong. Like standing up too fast from the couch. Or walking 'round with a fever.

Laura suddenly looks very concerned. Her lips form a wide O of surprise, and then she disappears as darkness sort of grapples with Amelia's head...

Shit.

She's fainting.

Amelia's gonna blame it on the head wound.

When she comes to again, she's wrapped up in Laura's coat, and it smells like heaven come down to earth. Laura's got one hand on the wheel, and the other on Amelia's shoulder.

"What'd I miss," Amelia asks.

Laura must have been tense, because suddenly she deflates. "Thank God. I thought you were...I was worried."

"Maldonados have hard heads."

"I'm aware."

She tries to twist in her seat to look around but regrets it and settles back against the cushion and her nice cocoon of Laura's coat. "Where's my car?"

"Back where you crashed."

"Where are we?"

The curve of Laura's smile then is intoxicating. The kind of endearing little thing Amelia could happily spend half her life trying to see again and again. "Not there," Laura says.

"You saved me." Usually, it's Amelia doing the saving of people.

There's a stiffness in the curve of that smile now. "I promised you I would."

CHAPTER 21

WHEN SHE WAKES UP AGAIN, the car's stopped, and she's all alone. Garish green light comes in through the glass from a big sign overhead. She has to twist to see the whole sign.

A motel.

They've stopped for the night.

Laura comes out of the lobby, slapping a brochure in her hand and looking somewhere between wildly irritated and exhausted. She opens Amelia's door without asking and then sighs.

"You're awake."

Very obvious.

She kneels by Amelia's seat, and her hand goes up to her hairline. "How do you feel? Dizzy still? Woozy?"

Amelia feels as if a tank parked on her head. She grumbles as much, and Laura ducks into the car to press warm lips to her temple. Amelia can't stop herself from leaning in to the touch.

Laura doesn't carry her to the room, but she keeps a hand around her waist and holds her close.

All it took to get her to cuddle was a little attempted murder.

She's real gentle as she puts Amelia to bed. She carefully removes her shoes before she brings the blanket up under her chin.

Then she pushes the one chair in the room in front of the door, sits in it, and stares at the door to the bathroom as if it'll burst open any minute and bad guys will come in with guns a-blazing.

"Can't be a comfortable way to sleep."

Laura's even got a gun out. A shiny looking pistol clutched in one hand. "Technically, I'm in the room next door."

"For appearances." Amelia assumes.

Laura nods.

"You're just gonna sit there all night?"

"If they come again, I want to be ready."

"I can think of more comfortable places to be ready from."

Laura's shoulders shift. "I'm half the reason for this mess," she says quietly.

Amelia just pats the few inches of mattress between her and the edge and gives Laura her best "come hither" stare. The one that got her labeled a sexpot for the whole summer of 1948.

That shatters a little of the resolve Laura's built since their reunion stopped being flirty and turned deadly. Laura trudges over to the bed as if she's headed down the corridor to the electric chair.

She's real careful about removing her shoes, taking each one off by hand and placing it on the floor at the foot of the bed. Then she goes and puts a pillow between 'em before she takes her seat on the mattress.

"Afraid I'll make a move?" Amelia scratches at the fluffy barrier between them.

Laura's gone prim. "Just being polite."

Amelia pats the pillow. "I don't bite."

"I want to keep my eye on the door."

If she's got her gaze on Laura and not on the door, it's almost easy to forget about the killers. She can almost wrap herself up in Laura's presence like she was wrapped in her coat earlier. She curls up into a little ball and hugs the blanket to her shoulders. "You really think they'll come?"

"We're no longer on a main road, and we're no longer headed north, so the odds are more in our favor."

"The gun probably helps."

"They'll be armed as well, and now that their first attempt didn't succeed, they might be—"

"More inclined to shoot me in the head."

"I'm sorry." It's a very sincere apology, as if Laura's to blame, which is fair. The timing of the original accusations is just too good to not assume Amelia's being targeted because she's Laura's "friend."

She rolls over and is careful not to look at her Sir Lancelot sitting next to her. Instead, she focuses on the ceiling. The paint was too thick when they painted and dried in globs.

"So twins, huh?"

Out the corner of her eye, she sees Laura blinking like she's taking a minute to catch up with the conversation. "Yes."

"Do they know what you do? For a living?"

"No."

"And Michel?"

"Of course he knows."

"But he doesn't work with you?" She figures that from the way people at the party fawned over him.

Laura laughs. "Despite his love of his adopted country, he's still very French. Just a diplomat."

Amelia's fingers play at the edge of her pillowcase, gaze on Laura again. "So you two had two gorgeous kids, bought that fancy home, and the rest is history." She wishes she had a cigarette. Or a drink. Or maybe some warm arms wrapped around her and soft lips pressing to the bump on her head. "It's a nice story."

Laura's gotten more and more stiff. Looking like the little stone Saint Francis in her ma's back yard. "Yes," she says quietly. "I suppose it is."

"I'm glad you started living in the world, Laura."

Laura stares straight ahead. She's on guard, waiting for the next goon to come through the door and try to murder them both.

"The thing is, I don't think I have." She says it softly. Almost quiet enough that, if Amelia wanted to pretend she didn't hear, she could. But Laura looks down at her, and Amelia knows she's meant to hear it.

And understand what Laura's saying.

There's a lot she's intimating with a few well-placed words. A lot that makes things complicated for Amelia. Laura too.

Amelia doesn't have the heart to tell her how romantic and stupid and impossible Laura's being. The woman's gone out of her way to keep Amelia safe, confessed she's miserable and alone, and now she's looking at Amelia with those dark earnest eyes. Wouldn't be right to go and call her an idiot.

She's woken up in a lot of arms over the last few years. Some smelling like cigarettes and others like fancy perfume and at least two that reeked of regret.

Laura just smells like Laura.

And maybe gun oil. Which is a very unique sort of oil smell and not so unpleasant on account of being associated with Laura.

Apparently, at some point in the night, she wrapped herself around Amelia like a python, gun still pointed at the door, and fell asleep.

Amelia twists around in her arms, until she's facing her properly, and pulls a lock of blonde hair away from Laura's eyes. Laura sleeps like she lives, with a frown making lines between her eyes.

The last time the two of them spent a night together, it was full of giggles and sex and bonding. Now, there's all this weight between 'em, and it's as if Laura's decided to carry it in that frown.

She presses her finger up to it as if a little pressure could smooth it out. Then she tucks her head in under Laura's chin and inhales her very particular and lovely smell and slips back into sleep.

She wakes up again, and she hasn't got a clue as to the time, but she's still wrapped up in Laura's arms. Only now Laura's awake, stiff as a doll, and looking at Amelia all stricken-like.

"I'm sorry," she utters.

Amelia snuggles closer. "Don't be. I can think of worse ways to wake up."

Laura slips her leg between Amelia's and reaches over to put the gun on the bedside table. It brings her close enough that all Amelia has to do is look up to place a kiss against Laura's pulse point.

That earns a sigh.

But Amelia figures she can do better.

She kisses her. Slow and easy and as casual as the waking up. Laura pulls her closer. Her head's nestled in the crook of Laura's arms, and they're kissing so lazily, she's inclined to check the clock and make sure it's not 1946 again.

All the girls Amelia's kissed over the years—the famous and the not so famous—none of them kiss quite like Laura Wright. She's got this way of pressing into a woman so that she's everywhere at once. Possessing her but with none of the manly idiocy something like that usually entails.

She's just holding Amelia. Not getting up to any kinds of business, despite the leg between her legs or the hand running lightly up and down her side. But it's as erotic as a dance and some fancy lingerie.

Quite unplanned, Amelia moans into Laura's mouth. Which works to get Laura all excited. Her thigh presses upwards into a bit of Amelia that doesn't need the friction but enjoys the hell out of it, and if they're not careful, they're gonna get naked and never make it out of the motel room.

She pulls back. "I'm hungry," she says.

Laura's lips are all red from too much kissing, her eyes are wide with confusion, and her mouth is working as if she's not sure if she should say "okay" or make a really well-timed come on.

"We should grab breakfast before they stop serving it."

Laura nods. "Okay." She kisses the corner of Amelia's mouth.

It's so easy that Amelia might just die from it. First, they both need to shower. Laura tries to say she'll use the shower in the room she didn't even sleep in, but Amelia glares until she blushes and uses Amelia's. While she waits, Amelia sits in front of the mirror and tries to brush the worst of the dried blood out of her hair.

Lady's got to love her if she was willing to kiss her looking like this. "I look an awful fright," she says when Laura emerges, hair damp and soaking the wide collar of her navy dress.

"Auburn looks good on you," she jokes and scrapes her nails along the back of Amelia's neck.

If she were to chronicle their kisses, record 'em in her diary alongside anecdotes about actors, then this kiss would get all the top marks. Laura's hand is on her neck, as Amelia cranes up to meet her. A curtain of wet hair surrounds them, damp, clean, and as pure as snow up on a mountain.

She gets out of the shower and creeps out of the bathroom. Laura's back in the chair, but she's moved it over by the bed so she can kick her heels up. Her back's to Amelia, and she's reading the James Joyce Amelia had in her bag.

Her publicist once asked if it was there to make her look smarter if her luggage was stolen, but she just likes his work. It's somehow easy to read. Relaxing.

Less so for Laura. Her brow's all wrinkled as she tries to suss out whatever's happening on the page in front of her, but she still hears Amelia's bad attempt at sneaking up.

"You know Gerard was always raving about Joyce, but I really don't see the appeal."

That makes sense to Amelia. Laura likes structure.

"Gerard. Was that…" She trails off, not wanting to actually say heavy words like "dead."

Laura snaps the book shut. "You two would have gotten along," she answers.

"Of course we would have. In love with the same gal, aren't we?"

She doesn't have a quick and easy answer for that one. She simply stares at Amelia as if she's grown a second head.

Score one for the ditzy actress. That score immediately tips back in Laura's favor when they sit down for breakfast. Over fried eggs, tomatoes, and toast, Amelia produces the "list." A group of people who are either pissed enough to set her up or now angry enough to see her dead before she can spill some precious secret.

She originally took a stab at the list while staying in DC, before the idea of being under surveillance scared her out of the city. She took another stab at it while Laura was showering that morning. The busy work was a good way to take her mind off the slippery, wet, naked woman just a door away.

Amelia figures that with all the duress she's been under and the big bump on her noggin, anyone would be impressed with the list she managed to put together. It's a really nice list.

Laura, being a career spy, is less impressed. "Who on earth is Rock Hudson?"

"An up and comer. In a lot of the rags right now."

Laura stops eating so she can reach over and cross his name off the list. "I don't think he's our fink."

"Montgomery Clift?"

Amelia shrugs.

"Kat—" Laura has to put the list down. "Why is Katherine Hepburn on this list?" She glances at it again. "And Joan Crawford? And... Amelia, Greta Garbo doesn't even go out in public."

She sips her coffee. "What we did wasn't fit for public." She really enjoys how flustered and jealous that makes Laura.

She grumbles. "I'd think half this list would want you dead just for making the list."

"You told me to make a list!"

Laura sighs. "Of people who might want to harm you. Not a list of every single person with whom you've had... dalliances."

"I'll have you know, every single fella on that list was above the belt."

Laura closes her eyes and takes in a deep breath that makes her shoulders rise and fall. "Right. So we're destroying this. Then we're going to make another less dangerous list of people you've royally pissed off."

"Better put Greta on that list too then." She thinks about it. "And Marlene."

"Dietrich?"

"Real mad."

"Is there anyone in Hollywood you haven't... engaged with?"

"Doris Day. Straight as a board and doesn't like you implying otherwise."

"Marvelous."

"Lousy singer though."

"Anyone who would legitimately want to hurt you? Besides angry European actresses you've loved and left?"

"Anyone who saw my turn in that Martin and Lewis flick?"

Laura rolls her eyes.

"I don't know, I mean my whole job is about making people like me. I'd be pretty lousy at it if I had a list of those who didn't."

"But there must be someone... men you've rejected? Studio heads you've infuriated. Actresses who lost out on roles?"

"Grace Kelly is doing just fine."

"What about the element you used to run with?"

"Spies who never call?"

Laura frowns. "The people with whom you used to rob banks."

"Setting me up as a communist spy's a little outside their purview."

She's kind of clueless as to who she knows that would want to torpedo her, and she doesn't want to talk to Laura about the big married elephant in the room. She figures if anyone really wants to send her up the river for being a communist it was the guy sharing a bedroom with Laura.

She sure as heck would have done something that stupid in his position, and she wouldn't have hesitated.

"Do we even think the guy who turned me in is the same as the one trying to murder me?"

Laura grimaces, but won't meet Amelia's gaze. "No. The man stupid enough to turn you in just kicked a hornet's nest. Didn't even think..." she mutters.

The man. That's what Laura says. And the grimace. And not looking at Amelia.

Laura knows exactly who set Amelia up as a communist spy.

She hasn't picked up on her minute slip and is still muttering to herself like a dotty old lady who gets mad when your dog pees on her tree. "Of course, doing something like turning you in for communism, would put you under scrutiny. Of all the high profile women in your... position, you're the one with the longest list of Washington elite on your dance card."

The "elites" again. "You think the folks trying to kill me have something to do with fellas like Chalmers," she asks.

Laura shrugs and stirs cream into her coffee. "Makes sense. You can't save yourself with a list of fellow communists, but this," her long finger stabs the list Amelia's made, "this would upend half the city."

"But I don't plan on actually making this list public."

"They can't know that."

"The whole reason I dated those men was because we could all be discreet. If one of us goes up, we all go up."

"And they think you're going up."

"So I tell 'em I'm not!"

All around them, people pause. A few keep staring down at their plates, while a few others crane their necks to look at her.

Laura purses her lips as if she's cranky with an unruly kid. "We should go."

Shit. Amelia nods. "Where? North?"

CHAPTER 22

WEST. THEY HEAD WEST. BECAUSE Laura insists that the men out to kill Amelia will be waiting at her apartment in New York and near her place in Long Island. "Wherever you were planning on going? They'll be there."

So they drive west with no particular destination in mind. It's a first for Amelia, who always has a plan—a goal—even if it's a bad one.

Every time they stop, Laura tells her she'll be "just a moment, darling" and disappears to make phone calls.

Amelia doesn't ask who she's calling because when they're driving it's as if there's a spell around the two of 'em. They don't talk about what could happen Monday, or Tuesday, or any day beyond the one they're living. Everything's easy in the immediacy of their escape.

Amelia doesn't want to break this spell that's come over them, and asking Laura who she's calling will do just that.

She doesn't want to point out how similar it is to forty-six either. As if the two of them can only be together when they're racing across the countryside, running from bad men in cheap suits.

That night, they stop in a rustic looking motor lodge at the foot of the Appalachians. The mountains don't look anything like Amelia's used to. There's no big hunks of stone jutting out of the ground and capped by white. Just walls of green trees that seem to go up and out forever.

They book just one room, unlike the night before. Laura insists on two beds and smiles at the boy who checks them in.

While Laura disappears to make more calls, Amelia mixes drinks for them in the room. Then drinks both of them and mixes two more.

Laura doesn't mention the calls when she comes back. Instead she sits on one of the beds, smokes a cigarette, and nurses her gin.

"Are you hungry?" she asks. "I'm hungry."

Amelia really doesn't want to eat. Not after the drinks. Not after the dread that's built in her since they checked in. She sips her drink and stares at the free newspaper on the coffee table. A church is having a festival tomorrow, and the Watkins lumber mill is still for sale.

"What if we never went back?" she asks. And she reaches over to idly flip the page on the paper. "Just keep driving."

"Well..." Laura stretches her legs out in front of her. "We'd hit the Pacific after a while."

"Could go south."

"That won't work," she says between sips. "Central America is just a hot bed of communists nowadays." She gesticulates when she says it, tumbler of booze still clutched in her hand.

"Why care? If I'm running, that'll be admission enough."

"But have you seen what communists wear? All gray wool and red? Better to fight them."

"For fashion." Amelia mock toasts.

"For fashion," Laura agrees. She finishes off her drink but never takes her eyes off Amelia. It's as if Superman's sitting across from her—with his fancy vision. X-Ray. Heat. It's all boiling up something inside of her.

Then Laura stands. Sets her glass on the table as she comes around it and stands in front of Amelia.

She's dead quiet as she carefully pulls Amelia up. Sets her glass on the table next to her own. Her hand splays across Amelia's waist. Fingers dig. Thumb moving in slow circles.

Her other hand sifts through Amelia's hair. Nails scratch her scalp.

She kisses her. Like gossamer. Gentle enough to be a dream. Kiss after kiss after kiss. Every press of her lips worrying away all the fears that have wrapped Amelia up.

It's all right she says with nothing but her touch.

There are no words exchanged. This, the two of them, is more than enough. Laura's cool fingers slip beneath the hem of Amelia's blouse, and Amelia's hand finds its way up to Laura's cheek, and all of that is enough.

To deepen things. To unfurl emotions—wants—that at least one of them has been very good at reining in.

Laura sucks in a long breath through her nose and tilts her head, and Amelia sinks into her, into the kiss, into the feelings she told herself were dangerous to feel.

Because until now it's been easy teases. Reminding Laura what she left, what she gave up.

But now...Now Laura's kissing her, and it's all Amelia could want. All she needs.

Her other hand presses against Laura's dress. Fingers lifting up against the center of her and rewarding Amelia with a delicious gasp.

All for her.

Because of her.

She grabs a handful of the dress, that sharp looking navy blue sheath, and pulls up. Just reaches down and finishes yanking her dress up to her waist. Laura never breaks the kiss—which has grown ravenous. Her hands are holding Amelia's face. Kissing her as if she's afraid Amelia might disappear in a moment.

Amelia slips her fingers around delicate silk panties and into a wanting warmth that makes her sigh.

Laura gasps at the touch alone. She breaks the kiss long enough to pant against Amelia's cheek. "Please."

Just for her.

She thrusts up, and the grunt and the needy pressure around her fingers—touching Laura like this is better than any profession.

Amelia pushes her back onto the bed and falls alongside her. Every ministration brings about some new gasp or keen.

She kisses Laura slowly. Teasingly. Draws the pleasure out of her like strands of sugar drawn out of something molten. Her chest hitches and she reaches for Amelia, her hand clumsy. She kisses Laura's palm. Nips at her flesh.

When Laura comes, it's fluttering breaths and a warm pulse against Amelia's hand. It fills Amelia with all kinds of wonder.

And Laura stares at her with what might be a similar kind of wonder. It could be, but only if they keep this moment long enough between 'em.

She kisses Laura's thumb as it grazes her lips.

This moment isn't gonna last. None of them can.

Because, eventually, they'll be back in DC, and Laura will have her family and her fears. Amelia will have the wreckage of her career, and the disaster that they might be together will be behind them.

So, she slaps Laura's thigh as if she's some kind of beast of burden and announces that she's famished and ready to eat a proper dinner.

She sees how confused Laura is as she saunters to the bathroom to clean up, and she's very careful not to apologize.

Because that would just invite the disaster they'll inevitably be.

They eat Oysters Rockefeller. Laura makes a joke about the real risk to their lives being consuming seafood so far inland. Amelia smiles pleasantly but doesn't laugh.

There are more jokes with the main course. Little self-deprecating asides. Laura tears herself down over and over again, always shyly watching Amelia for a response. A smile or a laugh or even a roll of the eye.

It's such a bizarre place for Amelia.

When they lived next door to each other, it was Amelia who pursued Laura, begging for scraps and praying for her to do nothing but stop by. Now she's the one sipping Old Fashioneds with a face set like a statue. She's making Laura work for something she knows she can't give her.

God, she's turned into an asshole.

"Did you always want children?" she asks.

An enormous asshole.

Laura stabs at her ham steak and seems surprised by the question. Amelia feels a little proud—on account of Laura being a fancy spy and all.

"I don't...I suppose I never thought about it... until I had them."

That's a lie. "Every girl thinks about kids." She's done with her own meal, a real steak that was too salty and green beans steeped in pork fat. She pulls a cigarette out and lights it. Orders another drink. "We start somewhere between learning to walk and potty training."

Laura's face is so still as to be unreadable. "Twice then," she finally admits.

"Gerard."

Laura nods. "And you," she says softly.

"Me?"

"We would have adopted. Officially they'd be yours."

"Like Crawford?"

"But more likable."

Fair.

"I'd keep a separate bedroom and be your 'good friend.' We'd periodically engage in high-profile romances with the most masculine men."

"John Wayne."

"Exactly. And we'd grow old. And fat. And happy. And your mother would love me despite my sex because there'd be grandchildren."

"Very important to her."

Laura nods, because yes, she knows how important grandchildren are to Ma Maldonado.

"Sounds as if you worked it all out. Was it you faking your death or marrying Michel that ruined the plan?"

It's meant to be a low blow, to spread around a little of the hurt Amelia's feeling, but Laura smirks. "Both, wouldn't you say?"

Didn't they order dessert? Amelia looks around for it. She's positive, even though she's about five drinks into her evening, that they ordered dessert.

"You hating me helps," Laura says conversationally. "As does this Wallace Beery impression."

Amelia sets her drink down. "I am offended."

"Your liver's probably more offended."

Her liver wants to punch her in the gut.

Cool fingers slip around her wrist and an insistent thumb sweeps across the inside.

They're in the middle of this nice restaurant. While her hair's changed and her makeup is different, she's still Amelia Wright, Oscar-winning actress on trial for treason. And Laura's holding her... looking at her... like a lover would.

She looks at Amelia, and the rest of the dining room doesn't matter. It's just the two of them again in a car riddled with bullet holes on the side of the road in New Jersey.

She can still hear the rain beating against the roof and see it slipping through cracks in the window.

"I'm terrified," Amelia says quietly.

"I know."

"Aren't you?"

"No. I've already done the most terrifying thing I can."

"What?"

"Leave you."

They don't stick around for dessert.

Amelia's not gonna look at the clock, but she knows it's later. Knows dawn's around the bend. And she knows she couldn't care less.

Laura's leaning against the headboard, sitting cross-legged with a cigarette dangling from her lips. She's got Amelia's list in front of her and is scanning it as if it's a bit of James Joyce.

Amelia runs her hand up and down Laura's thigh, real slow like. Drawing her nails across a plane of smooth skin that turns to goosebumps in her wake.

"I'm more partial to *Finnegans Wake*," she says, punctuating it with a kiss to Laura's knee.

"I know what you're partial to, and it isn't literature."

"I have diverse interests."

"I noticed. Not just American, but German, Swedish—Ow!"

So maybe Amelia bites her. It's not a real hard sort of bite. Just a light nip that has Laura yelping and tossing the list on the bedside table so she can scoot around to lean over Amelia.

"You bit me," she says.

"Very observant, Agent."

"Officer."

"Officer Wright." She squirms against Laura and gets the exact result she was looking for. A blush that starts on her cheeks and trails down her chest. "Plan to do something about it?"

Her lips—no, definitely her teeth—graze Amelia's lower lip, and Amelia's got to say that the feeling in her belly—one she's been having a lot this evening—is pretty fantastic.

Toe-curling almost.

And then it's shattered by a light knocking at the door that has Laura up with gun in hand so fast, Amelia's likely to confuse her with a character out of the funny pages.

She keeps both hands on her gun, barrel all steady and aimed at the door. Her hair's in her eyes, and she's stark naked, but Laura doesn't even notice.

If Amelia's heart wasn't about to beat out of her chest, she'd be just a little aroused at the sight.

The knock comes again.

"Closet," Laura snaps, and Amelia doesn't have to be told twice. She tosses Laura her coat just before she crams her naked self into the closet.

Laura shoulders the coat on, aim never drifting from the door. With coat closed, she moves closer. Flinches when there's another knock.

With a quick, worried glance back at Amelia she whips the door open and slips out into the hall.

Then.

Silence.

Well, not actual silence.

Amelia's bare-butt naked and huddled in a closet. Her breath rattles off the door and every minute shift seems to have her brushing against the hangers, which are loud as klaxons in the confined space.

It's not like being sixteen again.

Back then, all the waiting was done in a car, one foot on the gas, the other on the brake. Back then, the waiting was tolerable. It helped that she was always too dumb to really be worried. At least, she was before her brother lost his leg.

Back then, it was those same kind of nerves she got when she'd kiss a girl. She always felt light. Felt as if she was vibratin' full of something.

Now, sitting in a closet, the nerves are another kind. An anchor pulling the whole mess of her down into the floor.

She should get a gun. Or get Laura to get her a gun.

Then they'd both have guns, and she could learn to do more than close her eyes and squeeze the trigger and pray.

She ought to be able to do more than sit in a closet too.

With the boys, she was part of the plan. She cased the escape route and knew how to keep them alive.

With Laura, she's the damsel waiting in the wings, and she wants to wallop something with a bat.

Laura does come back. Eventually. Gun pocketed. Hair messier than before. Wearing a smeared shade of lipstick Amelia doesn't recall either of them having.

Followed by Judy goddamned Hayseed, smirking. And would you look at that shade of lipstick.

Amelia wraps her knuckle against the closet door because that's easier than yelling.

"It's all right," Laura says.

Amelia's pretty sure it isn't, but she steps out of the closet in nothing. "Wow," she says. "Judy Hayseed back from the dead. Wait till the other girls hear."

Judy has a tight smile that reminds Amelia of a rabid dog baring its teeth. "Amelia," she says too sweetly. "It's so wonderful to see you still alive. And still firmly in that closet."

Laura clears her throat. "Judy's been doing some of the legwork for me and has come to help out as she can."

Clearly been doing plenty of other things, too. Amelia feels like thumping herself because she never figured Judy for the lavender set, and she's usually real good at that.

"So you two… work together?"

Laura's got a look on her face as if she just farted. Judy smiles in a real irritating way. "Is that what she told you?"

"We haven't had a lot of time to talk about work. Doing other things."

"I know the feeling."

Now Laura closes her eyes.

And Amelia feels as if she's useless and back in the closet again. Also as if she wants to smack herself in the face. Especially with the way Judy—Judy from Iowa!—is smirking at her.

"So…" She claps her hands together. "Seeing as I've got to get up early and continue fleeing across country, trying not to get killed in the process, I'm going to go to bed. You two have fun with your little Hitchcock thriller, okay?"

She shoves 'em both out of the room and moves robotically to the bed—which doesn't look nearly as enticing as it did earlier. Especially the sticky spots.

God.

She's an idiot.

A big dumb idiot.

Judy from Iowa is some kind of hyper-capable spy, and Amelia gets paid to cry on command.

She hides away under the covers and reads the James Joyce to feel superior. A little later, she hears their voices in the hallway, followed by someone laughing and a door shutting.

She has to pull her pillow down on top of her head. Partly to avoid hearing any sounds she doesn't want to hear, but mainly just on the off chance that, if she dies, the assassin won't get to see how silly and mortified she looks.

But, when she's still not asleep because she's too busy in a pillow pity party, her door opens. And closes. When she peeks out from under her pillow, she finds a worn out Laura, gun drawn, trying to make herself comfortable in front of the door.

She calls Laura's name and feels a little less embarrassed when Laura freezes.

"I thought you were asleep," Laura says, rising back up.

"Too busy feeling like an ass to sleep."

Laura comes over to take a seat on the edge of the bed, her pistol settled in her lap. "You weren't an ass."

Amelia glares.

"You were a little bit of an ass. But it's been going around an awful lot lately."

She has to duck her head and grin because Laura's not wrong. She reaches over and scratches at the fabric of Laura's coat. "You gonna explain why you're camping on my floor."

"Judy thinks we're sleeping together."

"We are." She wants to act as if she gets it. She really doesn't.

Laura sighs. "And I don't trust her. Ever."

Oh. Right. She feels a little cold all of the sudden. "You think she's gonna kill me?"

"I don't know. I hope not." Laura can admit stuff like that casually. "But, Amelia, you must know, whatever her intentions might be, I won't let her hurt you."

"You've been making that promise a lot lately." Amelia says it reflexively. Not as if she means to hurt Laura. She just feels as if she's got to say it.

She regrets it when Laura flinches. So she reaches out before Laura can apologize or stand up, and she pulls her so she's half on top of Amelia. The gun ends up close to her head, and she's surrounded by the tang of gun oil.

She kisses her. All careful and slow. Just until Laura stops feeling so skittish against her.

"Might be safer if you're in the bed then—remember?"

Laura smiles against her lips.

They don't do anything more than kiss. A possible assassin one door over kind of cools any ardor Amelia might have lurking. But Laura does lie in the bed, and she pulls Amelia over until her head's resting on Laura's breast. She wraps an arm around Amelia and keeps the other close to that gun.

"I'm surprised," Laura says softly when they're both near passed out.

"What for?"

"You haven't ribbed me for clearly kissing her."

Amelia snuggles closer. "Cause hers isn't the room you're spending the night in."

"She was the one that kissed me."

"Laura."

"Amelia?"

"Shut up."

There's no faster way of feeling like an ass than waking up in bed, half naked, and a little bothered, only to find your lover fully dressed and sitting on a chair opposite you.

With her legs crossed.

Laura makes it a habit of making Amelia feel like the ass. She's clearly been up a while. Just sitting there. Waiting.

"This," Amelia motions to all of Laura, "is never a good sign."

"We're going back to DC."

Amelia sits up and hunches over the side of the bed, tugging at the half ruined curls of her hair. "We just left."

"Because we didn't have a choice. Now we do."

As only one thing's changed since the night before, Amelia asks, "Judy?"

"Judy."

"How does a former assassin change things? She gonna murder half of HUAC?"

It's the first time, Laura smiles, and it softens the hard lines of her face. "She'd like to. But I was planning on her staying at your hotel with you. If she's there, other assassins won't be. And while you're protected, I can sort out this mess."

"Sounds a little *Father Knows Best* to me."

"I'm very good at sorting."

"Right. You save the day, and I sit holed up in a hotel with an assassin. Can't say I like that plan."

"It's that or keep running. And we both know you don't run."

"Sure. Running is your forte."

"Amelia." Laura sounds so weary.

"I just...You come back into my life, tell me you love me, and you want to throw away your marriage to be with me. Then trouble shows up, and you're running again."

"I'm not running."

"The only difference is, you didn't dope the pastries—"

"It was coffee! And what exactly would you like me to do? *You* went and promised to out half of Congress. I have to find who's trying to murder you, convince them to stop, and then convince everyone else you've ever spoken to that you're not a threat. All while getting HUAC to drop the inquiry!"

"Yeah, that's a lot to do. Which is why you need help." She gets out of the bed. "So let me help."

Laura stands too. Only she looks as if she wants to run. She even turns away.

"Otherwise, what's the point," Amelia says. "It'll just be forty-six again and again."

"I won't fake my death—"

"But you'll leave me in order to protect me. It's what you're doing right this second."

"I'm really not."

"You're asking me to sit idly by while you save me." She comes closer but hesitates to actually reach out. Laura can turn skittish like a deer so easily. "I hate to break it to you, Laura, but I only play the damsel in the pictures."

"If anything we do goes sour—"

"We'll deal with it. Together."

Laura hangs her head. It's as good a victory as Amelia will ever get, tempered by Laura saying, "You're a fool."

Amelia slips her arms around Laura's waist, pulls her close, and presses a kiss to her shoulder blade. "A fool you're in love with."

Laura turns around in her arms, and her smile is broken. "Madly," she says, and she's being honest. Amelia can see it, can taste it in her kiss.

She squeezes her tighter as though just her arms and this promise will keep them together.

CHAPTER 23

THE CONVERSATION ON THE DRIVE back to DC is... lively. Judith sits up front, preens, and talks to Laura about their one common interest unrelated to sex or espionage.

Amelia, who's in the back seat reading—probably moving onto Proust—looks up with a raised eyebrow. "King Solomon's Mines? Really?"

Laura will not blush over her love of the movie.

Judith, being a fink, twists around in her seat to tell Amelia about how Laura just adores the movie. And the book. And the rest of that particular genre.

"Even Tarzan?"

"Especially Tarzan."

It's absolutely cutting the way Judith says it, with the quick glances down at the spine of Amelia's book.

Laura isn't an idiot. It's very obvious that Judith's attempting to piss all over her like her father's hounds used to piss on the trees around the property. But she can't just point that out. Judith operates on obfuscation and insinuation— just outright saying what one feels or thinks is the same as admitting weakness.

So, she announces that she also likes pie. And brandy.

Judith is flummoxed by the admission, but Amelia catches Laura's eye in the rearview and winks.

They all agree—without putting words to the sentiment—that there is one major person of interest in the plot to have Amelia murdered.

Her ex, Congressman Chalmers.

When they arrive outside his home in Georgetown, the pact of tacit agreement wobbles. Amelia feels she should go inside to help with the interrogation and blackmail. Laura disagrees, because while they've decided to do this together, she doesn't exactly want her lover seeing her interrogate a man.

It can be... uncomfortable.

Judith vocally doesn't care one way or the other.

"It'll be easier if you stay out here."

"What part of 'let me help' did you miss, Laura?"

"Oh no, by all means. Come inside while I rough up your ex. Maybe, if we're lucky, someone will get a picture and sell it to the papers. 'Big Lesbian and her Gal Pal Beat Off Congressman."

"Please leave the headlines to the professionals," Judith says.

"Agreed," Amelia says.

"It's smarter for you to stay in the car. Both for your physical safety—" Amelia starts to protest, but Laura doesn't let her. "And for you career."

"So it's safer for me? In the car? With the assassin?"

"Whom I'll kill if anything happens to you."

Judith nods. "It's true, if nauseating."

"Is that supposed to convince me? Because Rosie the Russian Riveter here isn't doing the trick."

She says her name plaintively. "Amelia."

Amelia relents. "Fine, I'll stay in the car while you torture my ex."

"I'm not... I won't torture him." Laura tried to pass it off as a joke. "Just scare him a little."

Judith looked idly in the direction of Chalmers's home. "He'll probably need to change his underpants afterwards."

Amelia doesn't look appalled by the idea. If anything she looks comfortable. Her gaze is warm with care, maybe—not concern. As if she might be perfectly okay with the dark and nasty parts of Laura.

In Laura's experience, the secret to a good interrogation is to minimize the physical pain inflicted, maximize the terror, and exploit the stupid. And lie.

With Chalmers she does all four.

"Got lousy locks on your windows," she says, and the man jumps five feet in the air and throws his hand to his chest dramatically. Then he looks dumbly around the room because if Laura's going to terrify a man into an admission of guilt, she makes sure the lights are off first.

He goes for the switch on the wall, and Laura tsks. "This is much more cozy, don't you think?"

"Cozy would be you getting the hell out of my house."

"I'm absolutely for that. Unfortunately, I can't leave until we have a little chat."

He sighs. "Someone sent you?"

"No. I took it upon myself to come here." She steps into a pool of light cast from a picture frame. The recognition is almost immediate for Chalmers.

His confusion comes a little slower.

She produces the list, stuck between two fingers. "Amelia made this. Your name's on it."

"I'm not a communist…" He's still woefully confused.

She clarifies. "But you'd love to bugger a few."

Everything, right down to Amelia being in mortal peril, is almost worth it for the face he makes as he moves from confused to absolutely bewildered. "How—why—Amelia sent a housewife to threaten me?"

"God, you're slow. I came on my own, you idiot."

"Why?"

"Because I'm on the list too, and I'm rather fond of its maker."

He sputters. "You're queer."

"As a three-dollar bill. Now can we get to the part where you agree to the blackmail I'm about to demand or are you going to keep looking at me as if I'm the idiot?"

Clearly, he prefers the staring and befuddlement, because he sags into a chair and rubs his head.

"Blackmail? How—"

She raises an eyebrow.

"How is it even supposed to work? If you out the list you out yourself."

"This is a romantic gesture, Chalmers. Because I only out all of us if she's hurt."

He blinks.

"As in, I'll have nothing to live for."

"What about Michel?"

She whips a vase off his mantle and throws it toward his legs. He quickly draws them out of the way with a yelp.

It's very satisfying.

"Good Lord. I honestly don't understand how you were elected to office. Can you at least acknowledge the present threat to your career and reputation?"

"I acknowledge the threat, but you forget, I know where you live too. I know your husband. And now I know your secret." He's so damned smug she wants to slap him. "You want to threaten me, girly, you better come with more than gumption and a list of fags."

He's right of course. Her reputation in most of DC is entirely related to her hostess abilities. Not her ability to kill a man six different ways with a fork. As far as he's concerned, he's being blackmailed by Lucy Ricardo.

She needs to prove herself.

So she saunters over, tips his chair onto its back, and straddles him. Lucy would never.

He tries to get her off, but between the gun pressed to the underside of his chin and the firm grip her legs have around his chest, he isn't so successful.

"You're confused, and that's understandable. So a little background on me, Congressman." She digs the sight of her pistol into his flesh. "In the war, I was responsible for the death of thousands of Nazi soldiers, and I personally killed over a hundred, many with my bare hands. Since the war, I've continued to put those skills to use as an officer of the Central Intelligence Agency and—and this part is very important Congressman—if a single hair is out of place on Amelia Wright's head, I will use those skills and my considerable resources to annihilate you and everyone you've bothered to ever care about." She lists them, because she's done her homework and would like him to know that too. "First it will be your cousin in Michigan. Then that roommate in law school that can't talk to you without blushing. After that, it'll be your dear father, you know the one you've been estranged from on account of your 'persuasions.' They'll be finished, one way or another, and if you're stupid enough to come for me directly?" She leans so close she can see the little black hairs on his nose. "I will see it coming, because you don't spend three years embedded in a war zone without being very good at identifying threats."

She pulls back the firing hammer on her gun. It's a particularly dangerous game. Semi-automatic pistols aren't meant to have their hammers cocked. The pressure required to pull the trigger drops to almost nothing. If Laura sneezes or Chalmers fidgets, he's dead.

It's the first time the two of them are on the same page.

"When," he swallows, and his stubble scrapes against the barrel. "When does this agreement start?"

"What?"

"I just want to know when your threat goes into effect."

"Now. It starts now."

"Then," he starts to smile, but it's the nervous smile of a very dead man, "we might have a problem."

Excellent. She plays dumb. "How? You don't know where Amelia is?"

"No, but I wasn't looking for her to begin with. I pay other people to do that."

"Who?"

"You've probably got a better idea than I do."

She does?

"They're from your agency."

She knocks him unconscious.

Her agency.

The CIA doesn't do ops in the US.

Okay, unofficially, they do ops in the US. Laura's done countless. But they would never be part of something so high profile. Unless they are as worried about the leak as Chalmers.

Which makes a little sense. Espionage tends to be popular work for people of hers and Chalmers's persuasion. It's all the lies. The queer ones learn how to lie faster than the normal ones.

But if there's an op, a secret op to ferret Amelia out by using Chalmers as bait, then they've had eyes on his home all night, maybe all weekend. Which means they saw her sneak in and didn't stop her.

Laura's done exactly what the CIA needed her to do. Deliver Amelia right into their hands.

She takes the stairs two at a time.

She has time.

They won't kill Amelia outside of Chalmers's home. They can't.

She crashes through the front door and bears witness to the end of a melee right there in the street.

There's a big dent in the rear driver's side door of her car from where a man was thrown into it head first. He's out for the count on the ground.

Judith, hat and coat still on, is huddled against the wheel well with a bloodied tire iron and another man by her side.

And Amelia—Laura watches a second car screech away.

Amelia's gone.

She'd scream, but she hasn't the time.

The gun in her hand is light as air, grip snug against her palm. She aims at the top of Judith's head.

It's as if she is walking on air. There's a vague buzz in her every step and a whine in her ear.

Amelia's gone.

"You had one job," she says. "You failed."

The head shakes as if Judith disagrees. She leans back against the car, and her head thumps against the metal.

And it isn't Judith lying against the car. The coat's too big; the hat's tilted wrong, and the hair's too dark.

"She had me change outfits when you went in," Amelia says. "Wanted me to be safe."

"They kidnapped the wrong woman?" She's supposed to be delighted, but honestly she's just confused.

Amelia nods. "Now come on. We got to go save the jackass."

The rescue involves a high speed chase. Amelia sails through traffic and pushes their car to its theoretical limits, while Laura hangs out the passenger window to take pot shots at the other car's rear window.

It's not very effective. The men who have Judith aren't going to blink about a little small arms fire. A machine gun or a high-powered rifle would be much more useful.

Thankfully, Amelia's behind the wheel. She can drive a damn car, and she wields the whole thing the way Babe Ruth used to wield a bat.

She darts between cars and ducks the few times the other car takes a shot at them. She doesn't talk. She's got incredible focus as she maneuvers a few tons of steel at high speed.

But she does smile.

A grin that lights up the whole car.

"This could be us," that smile says.

Every day.

Dodging bullets, using cars like knives, and saving the world and the girl.

It could be the two of them.

No hiding a whole chunk of their lives. No resignation and bitterness.

Just adventure. Together.

The other car slows, red rear lights fill the car with a macabre glow.

Laura wants to shout something like watch out, because there's only one reason they'd try to come up beside them. A reason Amelia would never consider. She's not a killer. She'd never slow the car down to come up beside the pursuit vehicle just to...

Shoot the driver in the head.

Laura screams Amelia's name. Reaches for her.

It happens too fast to do anything else.

The report of gunfire in so small a place booms.

Too damn fast.

Amelia jerks the wheel.

Glass shatters.

Their car crunches into the other. Metal shrieks as it's pried apart by the force.

Then.

Silence.

There's noise—she's sure of it—but in her head it hums like static on the radio.

Her head throbs, and when she looks around dazedly with blurred vision, she sees Judith in the other car, dislocating one man's shoulder and the other man's jaw. Finishing Laura's job for her.

"Did we get 'em," Amelia rasps.

"We helped. Looks as if—looks as if Judith is doing the actual getting."

"Great," Amelia says, but it comes out as a gurgle.

It's a very specific wheeze emanating from Amelia. It's dark in the car—too dark to see properly, but Laura doesn't need to.

Because she knows that wheeze. Has heard it before. When a blade draws across a throat to part vital elements of a life, blood and air mix. It's that wheeze.

There's glass everywhere.

The bullet missed its mark. But the crash. The glass...

She undoes her belt, fingers slippery with blood, and kneels beside Amelia. She presses her hand over the gash where blood wells up along Amelia's neck. She tells her it's okay, even though she doesn't believe it.

She begs her to hold on in the same breath that she tells Judith to run for help.

She begs her to stay. To live. To not leave her.

Amelia tries with all her might to obey.

And she lives, but Laura sits by her bedside and stares at the blood crusted under her own fingernails. The blame buries her, crowds around her until she cannot breathe.

It tempers the joy she should feel when Amelia finally opens her eyes and ruins the happiness when Amelia says, "Hey." It's reedy and raspy, and it means that Amelia is alive.

She kisses her hand, but nothing more. They're in a hospital, and people are eager to catch a sight of the actress nearly killed in a car accident. They crowd in the halls, offering an unintended layer of protection from anyone still seeking to murder her.

"You'll be happy to know," Laura's surprised by how rusty her own voice sounds, "that the inquiry has been dropped."

Amelia raises an eyebrow, and it stretches the streak of stitches across her neck and up her cheek.

"The press has painted you as an innocent, browbeat by Congress. They, and the public at large, are foaming at the mouth over the near loss of their little darling."

Amelia smirks.

"The list has been destroyed." Long, deep breaths Laura. "So, you are safe."

"You mean most of me. My best side's gonna look like shit on camera now."

It's a joke. Or meant to sound like one, but it makes Laura hunch over in her chair and hold her hand to her mouth.

Because, while she's been assured the scars will fade and Amelia will have a career again, she nearly didn't. The reminder of that near failure will be sketched into her skin forever.

And it's Laura's fault.

Amelia's hand, an IV jutting sharply out of it, curls around her wrist and gently pulls it away from her face. "It's okay Laura. I'm...I'll be okay."

Laura sighs and stands tall. Away from the bed. Just out of reach. Far enough away that Amelia would have to work to touch her with anything more than her leg. Amelia's face keeps threatening to pull into a frown, but being the Oscar-winning actress she is, she schools it into a mask instead.

One Laura can't bear to look at.

She stares at her nails. Something dark keeps finding its way underneath. "When you first refused to talk to me, I told myself it was because you were angry, and I thought, given time, it would all resolve itself."

She's not looking at Amelia, but she can picture the cocky little smirk. "It kind of did."

"And you nearly died, Amelia. You weren't just keeping me at arm's length because you were mad, but because you were brave enough to admit what I couldn't."

Amelia shakes her head. Opens her mouth to speak.

Laura holds her hand up. Not so high as to be an abrupt silencing gesture, but high enough to show Amelia she needs to continue to speak.

She has to.

It's just like plucking stitches, she tells herself. Quick and clean, and it will be over in no time.

"You're a tremendous actress with a career that puts you in the public eye, and I'm married, and a woman, and supposedly a spy."

She feels Amelia's gaze on her, bright and kind. Her hand's half outstretched toward Laura. Ready to argue. Always ready to argue.

"Michel was the one that set you up—do you know that?" She doesn't wait to hear an answer. "And he only did it because I invited you into our home. After I invited myself back into your life."

"I know."

Of course she knows. Of course she's figured it all out. Amelia's always been clever.

Laura closes her eyes so she doesn't have to look at her. It makes things easier.

"And the men trying to kill you? They were my colleagues."

Confusion clouds Amelia's eyes. "The CIA felt you were a threat and mobilized to deal with you."

"How can you know?"

"Chalmers. That's what he confessed to last night. He… They needed you dealt with."

"And now?"

"You're safe. Chalmers knows he can't go after you without things going very awry for him."

"So… we're safe?"

Laura laughs. "I wish that were true. We're safe as we can be, but the fact remains, you nearly lost your life, Amelia, because I invited you into mine."

"Laura." Amelia says her name with such weariness. So much fatigue. They've been dancing around this issue from the very beginning, and they always will dance around it. Unless one of them says no. Unless Laura says no.

She fidgets. Shrugs.

She has to put a stop to what they could be. For Amelia's sake. And this time…This time she has to be *strong*.

"You've always been so fond of calling us a disaster, Amelia. I've just finally realized you were right."

CHAPTER 24

WORK AND FAMILY. THE BALANCE has waffled a tad over the years, but the two have always been Laura's primary devotions. Oscar-winning actresses aside. Work and family.

They're a soothing routine she mires herself in.

She does not call Amelia.

She can't bear to reach out. Not after what happened. Not after what Amelia's endured under her watch.

So Laura returns to work and family, and she gets very, very good at one and fails miserably at the other.

Her boss, Frank Wisner, isn't happy about her involvement in the death of CIA assets, but when she tells him she has a list that J. Edgar Hoover and Joe McCarthy would give an arm for, he changes his tune and tells her what good work she's done.

"You knew her before, didn't you," he asks at the end of their meeting. Laura's packing up her things and preparing to go home early. "The actress."

She gives Wisner a loaded look, and his mouth drops open in surprise. "I don't understand it," he says, and he rubs the growing bald spot on his head. "But in her case, I almost do."

It's the most approval she could ever hope to get from Mr. Wisner. He tolerates, but he does not celebrate.

Things continue. Missions and praise and notes from Judith asking when they can work together next. She found the nightmarish road trip to be a "delightful romp."

At home, she is stiff and quiet, and her misery is never quite hidden.

It's Michel who finally looks at her from across the breakfast table and pulls the curtain away from her bit of awful theater. He simply says, "I think we should get a divorce."

The children are still upstairs, breakfast is on the table, and Laura's only just come in from work. There are dark circles under her eyes and every step she takes requires reserves she didn't know she possesses.

And when Michel speaks, it's as comforting as a hot bath.

She slides into the chair opposite him with a sigh and says nothing.

"You're clearly not... in this, and I like myself too damn much to suffer through it."

"Are you chucking me out?" She's prepared to fight if he is. Though she isn't sure she has the energy to do it in the present moment.

Perhaps there's a motor lodge nearby. She should really investigate that.

He shakes his head and shrugs. "No. I thought about it." He laughs darkly. "I got another home. One that's better for entertaining." Michel holds up a key ruefully. "Figure it's smarter to give you a copy than find one of your little children spies trying to break in." He puts it gently on the table and pushes it toward her.

She won't tell him it would be good practice for the kids.

Instead she takes the key and feels, perhaps a little, stunned. The divorce. The break up itself. Everything. She understood it was coming intellectually. It had to after what she's done. Yet, having a key in her hand, warmed from its stay in Michel's pocket, makes it all so much more tangible.

They agree not to tell the twins immediately.

They agree to keep things quiet.

He goes to work.

The children are taken to school.

Laura collapses onto the couch in her bedroom. It gives her a look into the half-empty closet.

He even took that old suit of his. The one that's too short in the legs.

She's muses on how efficiently he made his move until sleep grabs at her.

In her dreams, Amelia's sitting on the edge of the couch, and her hand is on Laura's cheek. She's forgiven Laura and asks why it is they have to be so madly in love.

Emphasis on the madly. She wakes up in her rumpled work clothes, and the clock on the bedside table reads after four in the afternoon. She realizes it was the squeal of her children playing in the backyard that woke her, and it drags her mouth into a smile.

She changes into pants and a button down shirt that's just a little too big and rolls the sleeves as she pads down the stairs barefoot.

The nanny's in the den putting away freshly polished silver Laura's grandparents insisted on buying them and looks startled to see her employer home and dressed down.

"She said you were home, but I didn't believe her," she mutters.

Laura raises an eyebrow. "She?"

"Your friend watching the children. When we got back from school, she was coming down the stairs."

Laura is sure a girlfriend just "popping over" is perfectly normal for many women. Unfortunately, most of her girlfriends were actual girlfriends, and nearly all of them have reasons to want to stab her with a knife.

She races through the house, her bare feet slapping on cold tile and plush carpets, and lunges out into the yard, just shy of breathless.

Then she stops. Her toes dig into cool grass. Amelia is there, sitting on a swing with sunglasses hiding half her face. Her high heels are piled with her purse on the ground, and she's smiling and playing with Laura's children.

She's here.

She must hear Laura, because she looks up sharply. Her whole head whips around. Her face is impossible to read with the sunglasses, but her smile is sunny.

Genuine.

The scars are fading.

She goes back to playing with the children, and Laura finds her feet carrying her over until she's sitting in the other swing with her son in her lap.

He's nearly too heavy for this sort of thing. He and his sister are both four and well on their way to five. His sister continues to play at pirate, jabbing a wooden cutlass at Amelia and shouting about what a "scurry-less bleeding landlubber" she is.

Laura should tell her daughter to watch her language, but her children are both so American they ride bald eagles to kindergarten, so she smiles and allows herself a measure of content and never questions why Amelia Maldonado is in her backyard, willingly playing house.

They dance around each other until dinner, smiling and chatting like the old friends the nanny assumes they are. Their hands sometimes touch, making Laura gasp and Amelia look away. It's all very quiet and reserved.

Then dinner comes. That's when the nanny, who has accidentally acted as chaperone, leaves for the night.

Suddenly, Amelia is looking at Laura with a poker face that would earn her a job in any spy organization in the Northern Hemisphere. She accepts the proffered drink with a soft "thank you" and is animated only when talking with the children.

With them, she's Amelia.

The glances at Laura, though, reveal some other mystifying and enthralling woman. At one point she winks at Laura, and she's so startled, her knee flies up into the underside of the table. The impact rattles her wine glass right onto its side.

When Amelia laughs as Laura mops up the mess, she's enigmatic.

It's maddening. Laura wants to ask why she's come. Amelia has declared they were doomed ever since the car they took broke down in rural New Jersey. She was particularly clear on her feelings in West Virginia when she whispered them between kisses, looking at Laura as though she needed her there and very far away all at once.

Laura's given her the out. She's let her know it's okay. She's made the sacrifice that was needed so Amelia could have a proper and healthy life.

But she's sipping her drink and behaving as mysteriously as any of the spies Laura knows. The sphinx gave Greek heroes less trouble.

"Do you need help getting them ready for bed," she asks after dinner.

Laura's son is already at the top of the stairs, and she's got her daughter in her arms, her knobby knees poking into her ribs.

"We'll be fine," she says quietly.

Amelia nods. Squeezes Laura's upper arm as though they're something. "I'll wait in the study then."

And she is. When the children are in bed and asleep, Laura climbs back down the stairs. Too softly, judging by the way Amelia startles when she appears in her line of sight.

She's lit a fire in the fireplace and poured brandy for the both of them, and until she sees Laura, she stares into that fire and seems to weigh all the troubles of the world in her head.

But then she snaps around and simply stares. So long that they both might blush.

"Hi." A greeting as oblique as Russian code when whispered by Amelia Maldonado.

Laura doesn't know what to say, so she takes her brandy and sits in the club chair opposite Amelia. The space between them seems like a chasm.

She nurses the drink.

Amelia breaks this second silence by cutting straight to the heart of things. "I have to say, before I got mad, I thought you were joking back at the hospital when you left." She peers at Laura. "Usually when you risk your life to save a gal, you don't up and leave her as soon as you got her."

"You were hurt because of me."

"I was hurt because a fella took a shot at me and broke some glass."

"And he took that shot because—"

"Hitler invaded France. Or screwballs in Congress like a witch hunt." Amelia shakes her head. "Laura, whatever part you think you played doesn't matter. If I want to blame someone, it's gonna be the guys who did the attacking."

"I'm sorry."

"I told you—"

"I know. I shouldn't blame myself. And I'm rational enough to understand that what's happened to you isn't my fault. But the fact of the matter is, you were in that car because I invited you into a war and then left you ill-equipped to wage it."

"So, when you showed up in New York, you should have had a rifle and some fatigues ready for me."

"No. I should never have invited you in the first place. There's a reason I left back in forty-six. You shouldn't have to fight this w—"

"And you should?"

"It's my job."

"Yeah. It's a job, Laura." She peers at her. "Not a life, and right now, it seems to me you're living it like it is."

"I have a family," she fires back.

"You do. You've got two gorgeous kids—"

"And—"

Amelia tilts her head. "And Michel left you. He called me a quarter of one to tell me."

"He was out of bounds."

"Probably. Think he's still stinging about how you'd rather spend a weekend on the run with me than a night in bed beside him."

"How?—"

"Day you left, I gave him a call. We've been chatting since. He feels bad about his part in nearly getting me killed."

"Bad enough that he just *gave* me to you?"

She laughs. "God no. He was ready to fight, but apparently you were so damn mopey, he couldn't handle it. Told me I'd 'won.'" She waves her hand with muted fanfare.

"That's barbaric."

"So is faking your death."

Damn.

There's a whisper of fabric, and then Amelia is kneeling in front of her.

"How did?—"

Her questions of how Amelia could possibly move so fast are stopped by brandy-brushed lips.

"Shut up and kiss me, Laura."

"I thought—"

Amelia's hand combs through Laura's hair, then pulls her close so they can kiss again.

And again.

And again.

Laura likes kissing. She does. And she likes sex too. She's had all sorts of partners and found a way to waste quite a bit of her life by doing nothing more than kissing another person.

But kissing Amelia is like coming home after the longest day. It's comfort and warmth.

And sweet. Even as ardent as Amelia is, kneeling between Laura's thighs and holding her close, hands tangling in her hair and teeth tugging at her lips. Even then, she's sweet.

Wonderful.

God help Laura, she loves Amelia Maldonado. In spite of all the very good reasons she shouldn't. In spite of how utterly impossible a relationship might be.

She loves her.

And not only desires her, but needs her.

Amelia's kisses stop much like the flow of water down the side of a house after rain. Her nose brushes against Laura's before she opens her eyes and smiles at her.

She's still close, her hand still in Laura's hair, but her fingers have relaxed and now just gently cup the back of her head. "There you are," she says. As if she's been searching for her. She darts in again for a quick, reassuring kiss. "You know I'm here because I'm crazy about you, don't you?"

Laura swallows, tries not to scan Amelia's face to sort out if she's telling the truth, and fails miserably.

One of Amelia's hands falls onto Laura's thigh, and her thumb moves in lazy, confident circles. She watches her hand.

Laura is quiet in her own confession. "I've been spending days trying not to be in love with you, reminding myself of how badly it could go. I kept telling myself we were a disaster, Amelia." She glances up and gives Amelia a sort of watery smile. "Then you tell me you and Michel broke up my marriage behind my back and all I can say is—"

"Thanks?"

"Disaster's a small price if I get to spend the rest of my days with you."

One day. Years later. Laura might regret what she said. Might consider disaster too high a price.

But that night, she curls up naked in the arms of the woman she loves and listens as her heartbeat drums steadily, feels the rise and fall of her chest, and thinks that disaster can try and wreck what she has.

But it'll have a helluva time doing it.

ABOUT MEG HARRINGTON

Meg Harrington is the author of several popular fic series online and lives in Brooklyn with her dog, her roommate, and two cats of indeterminate ownership. When she isn't writing about women loving other women, she's pondering the evolution of transformative art and working as a tech journalist.

CONNECT WITH MEG:
Website: www.meg-harrington.com
Tumblr: maggiemerc.tumblr.com
Twitter: @MegHarrington
E-Mail: meg@meg-harrington.com

OTHER BOOKS FROM
YLVA PUBLISHING

www.ylva-publishing.com

FOUR STEPS
Wendy Hudson

ISBN: 978-3-95533-690-5
Length: 343 pages (92,000 words)

Seclusion suits Alex Ryan. Haunted by a crime from her past, she struggles to find peace and calm.

Lori Hunter dreams of escaping the monotony of her life. When the suffocation sets in, she runs for the hills.

A chance encounter in the Scottish Highlands leads Alex and Lori into a whirlwind of heartache and a fight for survival, as they build a formidable bond that will be tested to its limits.

REQUIEM FOR IMMORTALS
(The Law Game – Book #1)
Lee Winter

ISBN: 978-3-95533-710-0
Length: 263 pages (86,000 words)

Professional cellist Natalya Tsvetnenko moves seamlessly among the elite where she fills the souls of symphony patrons with beauty even as she takes the lives of the corrupt of Australia's ruthless underworld. The cold, exacting assassin is hired to kill a woman who seems so innocent that Natalya can't understand why anyone would want her dead. As she gets to know her target, she can't work out why she even cares.

Book One in *The Law Game* series is a dark lesbian thriller with plenty of twists in its tale.

DELIBERATE HARM
J.R. Wolfe

ISBN: 978-3-95533-368-3
Length: 300 pages (70,000 words)

Ever since Portia Marks learned her fiancée Imma was executed in Zimbabwe, she's struggled with grief. Then a stranger tells her Imma is alive, but he's killed before she can ask questions. To learn the truth, Portia teams with two friends in the CIA. Her search takes her across continents and entangles her in a terrorist plot that will rock the globe. Portia's quest becomes a race against time.

CONFLICT OF INTEREST
2nd revised edition
(Portland Police Bureau Series – Book #1)
Jae

ISBN: 978-3-95533-109-2
Length: 466 pages (135,000 words)

Detective Aiden Carlisle isn't looking for love, especially not at a law enforcement seminar, but the first lecturer isn't what she expected. After a failed relationship, psychologist Dawn Kinsley swore to never get involved with another cop, but she immediately feels a connection to Aiden. Can Aiden keep from crossing the line when Dawn becomes the victim of a brutal crime?

COMING FROM YLVA PUBLISHING

www.ylva-publishing.com

UNDER PARR
(Norfolk Coast Investigation Story – Book #2)
Andrea Bramhall

December 5th, 2013 left its mark on the North Norfolk Coast in more ways than one. A tidal surge and storm swept millennia-old cliff faces into the sea and flooded homes and businesses up and down the coast. It also buried a secret in the WWII bunker hiding under the golf course at Brancaster. A secret kept for years, until it falls squarely into the lap of Detective Sergeant Kate Brannon and her fellow officers.

A skeleton, deep inside the bunker.

How did it get there? Who was he... or she? How did the stranger die—in a tragic accident or something more sinister? Well, that's Kate's job to find out.

BETWEEN THE LINES
(Cops and Docs Series – Book #3)
KD Williamson

Tonya Preston is a psychiatrist that likes dealing with her patients more than her family. Haley Jordan is a rookie police officer trying to find her way. They meet under dangerous circumstances that leaves a lasting impression. As their paths continue to cross, attraction simmers between them, but are they strong enough to power through the obstacles the people around them put in their path?

The Lavender List
© 2016 by Meg Harrington

ISBN: 978-3-95533-623-3

Also available as e-book.

Published by Ylva Publishing, legal entity of Ylva Verlag, e.Kfr.
Ylva Verlag, e.Kfr.
Owner: Astrid Ohletz
Am Kirschgarten 2
65830 Kriftel
Germany

www.ylva-publishing.com

First edition: 2016

Credits
Edited by Jove Belle, Gill McKnight and Jacqui McCarthy
Cover Design by Adam Lloyd
Print Layout by Streetlight Graphics

www.ingramcontent.com/pod-product-compliance
Lightning Source LLC
Chambersburg PA
CBHW020618260626
47157CB00003B/1066